THE
RED RIVER COLONY

A Chronicle of the Beginnings
of Manitoba

BY

LOUIS AUBREY WOOD

TORONTO
GLASGOW, BROOK & COMPANY
1915

The Red River Colony

Louis Aubrey Wood

BIBLIOLIFE

TO

MY FATHER

CONTENTS

ILLUSTRATIONS

CHAPTER I

ST MARY'S ISLE

WHEN the *Ranger* stole into the firth of Solway she carried an exultant crew. From the cliffs of Cumberland she might have been mistaken for a trading bark, lined and crusted by long travel. But she was something else, as the townsfolk of Whitehaven, on the north-west coast of England, had found it to their cost. Out of their harbour the *Ranger* had just emerged, leaving thirty guns spiked and a large ship burned to the water's edge. In fact, this innocent-looking vessel was a sloop-of-war—as trim and tidy a craft as had ever set sail from the shores of New England. On her upper deck was stationed a strong battery of eighteen six-pounders, ready to be brought into action at a moment's notice.

On the quarter-deck of the *Ranger*, deep in thought, paced the captain, John Paul Jones, a man of meagre build but of indomitable will, and as daring a fighter as roved the ocean

in this year 1778. He held a letter of marque
from the Congress of the revolted colonies in
America, and was just now engaged in harrying the British coasts. Across the broad
firth the *Ranger* sped with bellying sails and
shaped her course along the south-western
shore of Scotland. To Paul Jones this coast
was an open book ; he had been born and
bred in the stewartry of Kirkcudbright, which
lay on his vessel's starboard bow. Soon the
Ranger swept round a foreland and boldly
entered the river Dee, where the anchor was
dropped.

A boat was swung out, speedily manned,
and headed for the shelving beach of St
Mary's Isle. Here, as Captain Paul Jones
knew, dwelt one of the chief noblemen of the
south of Scotland. The vine-clad, rambling
mansion of the fourth Earl of Selkirk was just
behind the fringe of trees skirting the shore.
According to the official report of this descent
upon St Mary's Isle, it was the captain's
intention to capture Selkirk, drag him on
board the *Ranger*, and carry him as a hostage
to some harbour in France. But it is possible
that there was another and more personal
object. Paul Jones, it is said, believed that
he was a natural son of the Scottish nobleman,

and went with this armed force to disclose his identity.

When the boat grated upon the shingle the seamen swarmed ashore and found themselves in a great park, interspersed with gardens and walks and green open spaces. The party met with no opposition. Everything, indeed, seemed to favour their undertaking, until it was learned from some workmen in the grounds that the master was not at home.

In sullen displeasure John Paul Jones paced nervously to and fro in the garden. His purpose was thwarted ; he was cheated of his prisoner. A company of his men, however, went on and entered the manor-house. There they showed the hostile character of their mission. Having terrorized the servants, they seized the household plate and bore it in bags to their vessel. Under full canvas the *Ranger* then directed her course for the Irish Sea.

Thomas Douglas, the future lord of the Red River Colony, was a boy of not quite seven years at the time of this raid on his father's mansion. He had been born on June 20, 1771, and was the youngest of seven brothers in the Selkirk family. What he thought of Paul Jones and his marauders can only be surmised. St Mary's Isle was a remote spot, replete with relics of history, but uneventful in daily life ; and a real adventure at his own doors could hardly fail to leave an impression on the boy's mind. The historical associations of St Mary's Isle made it an excellent training-ground for an imaginative youth. Monks of the Middle Ages had noted its favourable situation for a religious community, and the canons-regular of the Order of St Augustine had erected there one of their priories. A portion of an extensive wall which had surrounded the cloister was retained in the Selkirk manor-house. Farther afield were other reminders of past days to stir the imagination of young Thomas Douglas. A few miles eastward from his home was Dundrennan Abbey. Up the Dee was Thrieve Castle, begun by Archibald the Grim, and later used as a stronghold by the famous Black Douglas.

The ancient district of Galloway, in which the Selkirk home was situated, had long been known as the Whig country. It had been the chosen land of the Covenanters, the foes of privilege and the defenders of liberal principles in government. Its leading families, the Kennedys, the Gordons, and

the Douglases, formed a broad-minded aristo-
cracy. In such surroundings, as one of the
' lads of the Dee,' Thomas Douglas inevitably
developed a type of mind more or less radical.
His political opinions, however, were guided
by a cultivated intellect. His father, a patron
of letters, kept open house for men of genius,
and brought his sons into contact with some
of the foremost thinkers and writers of the
day. One of these was Robert Burns, the
most beloved of Scottish poets. In his earlier
life, when scarcely known to his countrymen,
Burns had dined with Basil, Lord Daer,
Thomas Douglas's eldest brother and heir-
apparent of the Selkirk line. This was the
occasion commemorated by Burns in the
poem of which this is the first stanza :

> This wot ye all whom it concerns :
> I, Rhymer Robin, alias Burns,
>   October twenty-third,
> A ne'er-to-be-forgotten day,
> Sae far I sprachl'd up the brae
>   I dinner'd wi' a Lord.

One wet evening in the summer of 1793 Burns
drew up before the Selkirk manor-house in
company with John Syme of Ryedale. The
two friends were making a tour of Galloway
on horseback. The poet was in bad humour.

The night before, during a wild storm of rain and thunder, he had been inspired to the rousing measures of ' Scots wha hae wi' Wallace bled.' But now he was drenched to the skin, and the rain had damaged a new pair of jemmy boots which he was wearing. The passionate appeal of the Bruce to his country-men was now forgotten, and Burns was as cross as the proverbial bear. It was the dinner hour when the two wanderers arrived and were cordially invited to stay. Various other guests were present ; and so agreeable was the company and so genial the welcome, that the grumbling bard soon lost his irrit-able mood. The evening passed in song and story, and Burns recited one of his ballads, we are told, to an audience which listened in ' dead silence.' The young mind of Thomas Douglas could not fail to be influenced by such associations.

In 1786 Thomas Douglas entered the Uni-versity of Edinburgh. From this year until 1790 his name appears regularly upon the class lists kept by its professors. The ' grey metropolis of the North ' was at this period pre-eminent among the literary and academic centres of Great Britain. The principal of the university was William Robertson, the celebrated historian. Professor Dugald Stewart, who held the chair of philosophy, had gained a reputation extending to the continent of Europe. Adam Smith, the epoch-making economist, was spending the closing years of his life at his home near the Canongate churchyard. During his stay in Edinburgh, Thomas Douglas interested himself in the work of the literary societies, which were among the leading features of academic life. At the meetings essays were read upon various themes and lengthy debates were held. In 1788 a group of nineteen young men at Edinburgh formed a new society known as ' The Club.' Two of the original members were Thomas Douglas and Walter Scott, the latter an Edinburgh lad a few weeks younger than Douglas. These two formed an intimate friendship which did not wane when one had become a peer of the realm, his mind occupied by a great social problem, and the other a baronet and the greatest novelist of his generation.

When the French Revolution stirred Europe to its depths, Thomas Douglas was attracted by the doctrines of the revolutionists, and went to France that he might study the new movement. But Douglas, like so many of his contemporaries in Great Britain, was filled with disgust at the blind carnage of the Revolution. He returned to Scotland and began a series of tours in the Highlands, studying the conditions of life among his Celtic countrymen and becoming proficient in the use of the Gaelic tongue.   Not France but Scotland was to be the scene of his reforming efforts.

CHAPTER II

SELKIRK, THE COLONIZER

FROM the north and west of Scotland have come two types of men with whom every schoolboy is now familiar. One of these has been on many a battlefield. He is the brawny Highland warrior, with buckled tartan flung across his shoulder, gay in pointed plume and filibeg. The other is seen in many a famous picture of the hill-country—the Highland shepherd, wrapped in his plaid, with staff in hand and long-haired dog by his side, guarding his flock in silent glen, by still-running burn, or out upon the lonely brae.

But in Thomas Douglas's day such types of Highland life were very recent factors in Scottish history. They did not appear, indeed, until after the battle of Culloden and the failure of the Rebellion of 1745. Loyalty, firm and unbending, has always been a characteristic of the mountaineer. The Highlanders held to the ancient house of Stuart which had been dethroned. George II of England was repudiated by most of them as a 'wee, wee German Lairdie.' More than thirty thousand claymores flashed at the beck of Charles Edward, the Stuart prince, acclaimed as 'King o' the Highland hearts.' When the uprising had been quelled and Charles Edward had become a fugitive with a price on his head, little consideration could be expected from the house of Hanover. The British government decided that, once and for all, the power of the clans should be broken.

For centuries the chief strength of the Highland race had lain in the clan. By right of birth every Highlander belonged to a sept or clan. His overlord was an elected chief, whom he was expected to obey under all circumstances. This chief led in war and exercised a wide authority over his people. Just below him were the tacksmen, who were more nearly related to him than were the ordinary clansmen. Every member of the clan had some land; indeed, each clansman had the same rights to the soil as the chief himself enjoyed. The Highlander dwelt in a humble shealing; but, however poor, he gloried in his independence. He grew his own corn and took it to the common mill; he raised fodder for his black, shaggy cattle which roamed upon the rugged hillsides or in the misty valleys; his women-folk carded wool sheared from his own flock, spun it, and wove the cloth for bonnet, kilt, and plaid. When his chief had need of him, the summons was vivid and picturesque. The Fiery Cross was carried over the district by swift messengers who shouted a slogan known to all; and soon from every quarter the clansmen would gather at the appointed meeting-place.

The clans of the Highlands had led a wild, free life, but their dogged love for the Stuart cause brought to them desolation and ruin. By one stroke the British government destroyed the social fabric of centuries. From the farthest rock of the storm-wasted Orkneys to the narrow home of Clan Donald in Argyllshire, the ban of the government was laid on the clan organization. Worst of all, possession of the soil was given, not to the many clansmen, but to the chiefs alone.

While the old chiefs remained alive, little real hardship was inflicted. They were wedded to the old order of things, and left it unchanged. With their successors, however, began a new era. These men had come under the influence of the south, whither they had gone for education, to correct the rudeness of their Highland manners. On their return to their native country they too often held themselves aloof from the uncouth dwellers in the hills. The mysterious love of the Gael for his kith and kin had left them ; they were no longer to their dependants as fathers to children. More especially had these Saxon-bred lordlings fallen a prey to the commercial ideas of the south. It was trying for them to possess the nominal dignity of landlords without the money needed to maintain their rank. They were bare of retinue, shabby in equipage, and light of purse. They saw but one solution of their difficulty. Like their English and Lowland brethren, they must increase the rents upon their Highland estates. So it came about that the one-time clansmen, reduced to mere tenants, groaned for the upkeep of their overlords.

Nor did this end the misfortunes of the clansmen. An attractive lure was held out to the new generation of chieftains, and greed and avarice were to triumph. Southern speculators had been rambling over the Highlands, eager to exploit the country. These men had seen a land of grass and heather, steep crag, and winter snow. Observing that the country was specially adapted to the raising of sheep, they sought by offering high rents to acquire land for sheep-walks. Thus, through the length and breadth of the Highlands, great enclosures were formed for the breeding of sheep. Where many crofters had once tilled the soil, only a lone shepherd was now found, meditating on scenes of desolation. Ruined dwellings and forsaken hamlets remained to tell the tale. Human beings had been evicted : sheep had become the ' devourers of men.' In many parts of the Highlands the inhabitants, driven from mountain homes, were forced to eke out a meagre existence on narrow strips of land by the seashore, where they pined and where they half-starved on the fish caught in the dangerous waters.

From such a dilemma there was but one escape. Behind the evicted tenantry were the sheep-walks ; before them was the open sea. Few herrings came to the net ; the bannock meal was low ; the tartan threadbare. In their utter hopelessness they listened to the good news which came of a land beyond the

Atlantic where there was plenty and to spare. It is small wonder that as the ships moved westward they carried with them the destitute Highlander, bound for the colonies planted in North America.

This ' expatriation ' was spread over many weary years. It was in full process in 1797, when Thomas Douglas became Lord Daer. His six elder brothers had been ailing, and one by one they had died, until he, the youngest, alone survived. Then, when his father also passed away, on May 24, 1799, he was left in possession of the ancestral estates and became the fifth Earl of Selkirk.

As a youngest son, who would have to make his own way in the world, Thomas Douglas had prepared himself, and this was a distinct advantage to him when his elevation in rank occurred. He entered into his fortune and place an educated man, with the broad outlook upon life and the humanitarian sympathy which study and experience bring to a generous spirit. Now he was in a position to carry out certain philanthropic schemes which had begun earlier to engage his attention. His jaunts in the Highlands amid ' the mountain and the flood ' were now to bear fruit. The dolorous plaint of the hapless clansmen had

struck an answering chord in the depths of his
nature. As Thomas Douglas, he had meant
to interest himself in the cause of the Highlanders; now that he was Earl of Selkirk, he
decided, as a servant of the public, to use
his wealth and influence for their social and
economic welfare. With this resolve he took
up what was to be the main task of his life—
the providing of homes under other skies for
the homeless in the Highlands.

In the spring of 1802 the young earl
addressed a letter to Lord Pelham, a minister
in the British government, in which he dwelt
with enthusiasm upon the subject of emigration. His letter took the form of an appeal,
and was prophetic. There had previously
come into Selkirk's hands Alexander Mackenzie's thrilling story of his journeys to the
Arctic and the Pacific. This book had filled
Selkirk's mind with a great conception. Men
had settled, he told Lord Pelham, on the
sea-coast of British America, until no tract
there was left uninhabited—but frozen wastes
and arid plains. What of the fruitful regions
which lay in the vast interior ? It was
thither that the government should turn the
thoughts of the homeless and the improvident.
Leading to this temperate and fertile area was

an excellent northern highway—the waters of Hudson Bay and the Nelson.

Lord Selkirk received a not unfavourable reply to his appeal. The authorities said that, though for the present they could not undertake a scheme of emigration such as he had outlined, they would raise no barrier against any private movement which Lord Selkirk might care to set on foot. The refusal of the government itself to move the dispossessed men was dictated by the political exigencies of the moment. Great Britain had no desire to decrease her male population. Napoleon had just become first consul in France. His imperial eagles would soon be carrying their menace across the face of Europe, and Great Britain saw that, at any moment, she might require all the men she could bring into the field.

As the government had not discountenanced his plan, the Earl of Selkirk determined to put his theories at once into practice. He made known in the Highlands that he proposed to establish a settlement in British North America. Keen interest was aroused, and soon a large company, mostly from the isle of Skye, with a scattering from other parts of Scotland, was prepared to embark.

It was intended that these settlers should sail for Hudson Bay. This and the lands beyond were, however, by chartered right the hunting preserve of the Hudson's Bay Company, of which more will be said. Presumably this company interfered, for unofficial word came from England to Selkirk that the scheme of colonizing the prairie region west of Hudson Bay and the Great Lakes would not be pleasing to the government. Selkirk, however, quickly turned elsewhere. He secured land for his settlers in Prince Edward Island, in the Gulf of St Lawrence. The prospective colonists, numbering eight hundred, sailed from Scotland on board three chartered vessels, and reached their destination in the midsummer of 1803.

Lord Selkirk had intended to reach Prince Edward Island in advance of his colonists, in order to make ready for their arrival. But he was delayed by his private affairs, and when he came upon the scene of the intended settlement, after sunset on an August day, the ships had arrived and one of them had landed its passengers. On the site of a little French village of former days they had propped poles together in a circle, matted them with foliage from the trees, and were

living, like a band of Indians, in these im-
provised wigwams.

There was, of course, much to be done.
Trees and undergrowth had to be cleared away,
surveys made, and plots of land meted out to
the various families.   Lord Selkirk remained
for several weeks supervising the work.   Then,
leaving the colony in charge of an agent, he
set out to make a tour of Canada and the
United States.

Meanwhile, Selkirk's agents in Scotland
were not idle.   During the same summer
(1803) a hundred and eleven emigrants were
mustered at Tobermory, a harbour town on
the island of Mull.   Most of them were natives
of the island.   For some reason, said to be
danger of attack by French privateers, they
did not put out into the Atlantic that year;
they sailed round to Kirkcaldy and wintered
there.   In May 1804 the party went on board
the ship *Oughton* of Greenock, and after a six
weeks' journey landed at Montreal.   Thence
they travelled in bateaux to Kingston.

These settlers were on their way to Baldoon
Farm, a tract of about nine hundred and fifty
acres which Lord Selkirk had purchased for
them in Upper Canada, near Lake St Clair.
Selkirk himself met the party at Kingston,

having journeyed from Albany for that purpose. He brought with him an Englishman named Lionel Johnson and his family. The new settlement was to be stocked with a thousand merino sheep, already on the way to Canada, and Johnson was engaged to take care of these and distribute them properly among the settlers   The journey from Kingston to the Niagara was made in a good sailing ship and occupied only four days.   The goods of the settlers were carried above the Falls. Then the party resumed their journey along the north shore of Lake Erie in bateaux, and arrived at their destination in September.

Baldoon Farm was an ill-chosen site for a colony.   The land, prairie-like in its appearance, lay in what is now known as the St Clair Flats in Kent county, Ontario.   It proved to be too wet for successful farming.   It was with difficulty, too, that the settlers became inured to the climate.   Within a year forty-two are reported to have died, chiefly of fever and dysentery.   The colony, however, enjoyed a measure of prosperity until the War of 1812 broke out, when the Americans under General M'Arthur, moving from Detroit, despoiled it of stores, cattle, and sheep, and almost obliterated it.   In 1818 Lord Selkirk sold the land to John M'Nab, a trader of the Hudson's Bay Company. Many descendants of the original settlers are, however, still living in the neighbourhood.

Before returning to Great Britain, Lord Selkirk rested from his travels for a time in the city of Montreal, where he was fêted by many of the leading merchants. What the plutocrats of the fur trade had to relate to Selkirk was of more than passing interest. No doubt he talked with Joseph Frobisher in his quaint home on Beaver Hall Hill. Simon M'Tavish, too, was living in a new-built mansion under the brow of Mount Royal. This ' old lion of Montreal,' who was the founder of the North-West Company, had for the mere asking a sheaf of tales, as realistic as they were entertaining. Honour was done Lord Selkirk during his stay in the city by the Beaver Club, which met once a fortnight. This was an exclusive organization, which limited its membership to those who dealt in furs. Every meeting meant a banquet, and at these meetings each club-man wore a gold medal on which was engraved the motto, ' Fortitude in Distress.' Dishes were served which smacked of prairie and forest—venison, bear flesh, and

PLACE D'ARMES, MONTREAL, IN 1807

From a water-colour sketch after Dillon in McGill University Library

buffalo tongue. The club's resplendent glass and polished silver were marked with its crest, a beaver. After the toasts had been drunk, the jovial party knelt on the floor for a final ceremony. With pokers or tongs or whatever else was at hand, they imitated paddlers in action, and a chorus of lusty voices joined in a burst of song. It may be supposed that Lord Selkirk was impressed by what he saw at this gathering and that he was a sympathetic guest. He asked many questions, and nothing escaped his eager observation. Little did he then think that his hosts would soon be banded together in a struggle to the death against him and his schemes of western colonization.

CHAPTER III

THE PURSE-STRINGS LOOSEN

TRAFFIC in furs was hazardous, but it brought great returns. The peltry of the north, no less than the gold and silver of the south, gave impetus to the efforts of those who first settled the western hemisphere. In expectation of ample profits, the fur ship threaded its way through the ice-pack of the northern seas, and the trader sent his canoes by tortuous stream and toilsome portage. In the early days of the eighteenth century sixteen beaver skins could be obtained from the Indians for a single musket, and ten skins for a blanket. Profits were great, and with the margin of gain so enormous, jealousies and quarrels without number were certain to arise between rival fur traders.

The right to the fur trade in America had been granted—given away, as the English of the time thought—by the hand of Charles II of England. In prodigal fashion Charles con-

JOSEPH FROBISHER, A PARTNER IN THE
NORTH-WEST COMPANY

ceded, in 1670, a charter, which conveyed extensive lands, with the privileges of monopoly, to the ' Company of Adventurers of England trading into Hudson's Bay.' But if the courtiers of the Merry Monarch had any notion that he could thus exclude all others from the field, their dream was an empty one. England had an active rival in France, and French traders penetrated into the region granted to the Hudson's Bay Company. Towards the close of the seventeenth century Le Moyne d'Iberville was making conquests on Hudson Bay for the French king, and Greysolon Du Lhut was carrying on successful trading operations in the vicinity of Lakes Nipigon and Superior. Even after the Treaty of Utrecht (1713) had given the Hudson Bay territories to the English, the French-Canadian explorer La Vérendrye entered the forbidden lands, and penetrated to the more remote west. A new situation arose after the British conquest of Canada during the Seven Years' War. Plucky independent traders, mostly of Scottish birth, now began to follow the watercourses which led from the rapids of Lachine on the St Lawrence to the country beyond Lake Superior. These men treated with disdain the royal charter of the Hudson's

Bay Company. In 1783 a group of them
united to form the North-West Company, with
headquarters at Montreal. The organization
grew in strength and became the most powerful antagonist of the older company, and the
open feud between the two spread through
the wide region from the Great Lakes to the
slopes of the Rocky Mountains.

The Nor'westers, as the partners and
servants of the North-West Company were
called, were bold competitors. Their enthusiasm for the conflict was all the more
eager because their trade was regarded as
illicit by their rivals. There was singleness
of purpose in their ranks ; almost every man
in the service had been tried and proved. All
the Montreal partners of the company had
taken the long trip to the Grand Portage, a
transit station at the mouth of the Pigeon
river, on the western shore of Lake Superior.
Other partners had wintered on the frozen
plains or in the thick of the forest, tracking
the yellow-grey badger, the pine-marten, and
the greedy wolverine. The guides employed
by the company knew every mile of the rivers,
and they rarely mistook the most elusive trail.
Its interpreters could converse with the red
men like natives. . Even the clerks who looked

after the office routine of the company laboured with zest, for, if they were faithful and attentive in their work, the time would come when they, too, would be elected as partners in the great concern. The canoemen were mainly French-Canadian coureurs de bois, gay voyageurs on lake and stream. In the veins of many of them flowed the blood of Cree or Iroquois. Though half barbarous in their mode of life, they had their own devotions. At the first halting-place on their westward journey, above Lachine, they were accustomed to enter a little chapel which stood on the bank of the Ottawa. Here they prayed reverently that ' the good Saint Anne,' the friend of all canoemen, would guard them on their way to the Grand Portage. Then they dropped an offering at Saint Anne's shrine, and pointed their craft against the current. These rovers of the wilderness were buoyant of heart, and they lightened the weary hours of their six weeks' journey with blithe songs of love and the river. When the snow fell and ice closed the river, they would tie their ' husky ' dogs to sledges and travel over the desolate wastes, carrying furs and provisions.

It was a very different company that traded into Hudson Bay. The Hudson's Bay Company was launched on its career in a princely manner, and had tried to cling fast to its time-worn traditions. The bundles of uncured skins were received from the red men by its servants with pomp and dignity. At first the Indians had to bring their 'catch' to the shores of Hudson Bay itself, and here they were made to feel that it was a privilege to be allowed to trade with the company. Some-times they were permitted to pass in their wares only through a window in the outer part of the fort. A beaver skin was the re-gular standard of value, and in return for their skins the savages received all manner of gaudy trinkets and also useful merchandise, chiefly knives, hatchets, guns, ammunition, and blankets. But before the end of the eighteenth century the activity of the Nor'-westers had forced the Hudson's Bay Com-pany out of its aristocratic slothfulness. The savages were now sought out in their prairie homes, and the company began to set up trading-posts in the interior, all the way from Rainy Lake to Edmonton House on the North Saskatchewan.

Such was the situation of affairs in the fur-bearing country when the Earl of Selkirk had his vision of a rich prairie home for the desolate Highlanders. Though he had not himself visited the Far West, he had some conception of the probable outcome of the fierce rivalry between the two great fur companies in North America. He foresaw that, sooner or later, if his scheme of planting a colony in the interior was to prosper, he must ally himself with one or the other of these two factions of traders.

We may gain a knowledge of Lord Selkirk's ideas at this time from his own writings and public utterances. In 1805 he issued a work on the Highlands of Scotland, which Sir Walter Scott praised for its ' precision and accuracy,' and which expressed the significant sentiment that the government should adopt a policy that would keep the Highlanders within the British Empire. In 1806, when he had been chosen as one of the sixteen representative peers from Scotland, he delivered a speech in the House of Lords upon the subject of national defence, and his views were afterwards stated more fully in a book. With telling logic he argued for the need of a local militia, rather than a volunteer force, as the best protection for England in a moment of peril. The tenor of this and Selkirk's other writings would indicate the staunchness of his patriotism. In his efforts at colonization his desire was to keep Britain's sons from emigrating to an alien shore.

'Now, it is our duty to befriend this people,' he affirmed, in writing of the Highlanders. 'Let us direct their emigration ; let them be led abroad to new possessions.' Selkirk states plainly his reason. 'Give them homes under our own flag,' is his entreaty, 'and they will strengthen the empire.'

In 1807 Selkirk was chosen as lord-lieu-tenant of the stewartry of Kirkcudbright, and in the same year took place his marriage with Jean Wedderburn-Colvile, the only daughter of James Wedderburn-Colvile of Ochiltree. One year later he was made a Fellow of the Royal Society, a distinction conferred only upon intellectual workers whose labours have increased the world's stock of knowledge.

After some shrewd thinking Lord Selkirk decided to throw in his lot with the Hudson's Bay Company. Why he did this will subse-quently appear. At first, one might have judged the step unwise. The financiers of London believed that the company was drift-ing into deep water. When the books were made up for 1808, there were no funds avail-able for dividends, and bankruptcy seemed inevitable. Any one who owned a share of Hudson's Bay stock found that it had not earned him a sixpence during that year. The company's business was being cut down by the operations of its aggressive rival. The chief cause, however, of the company's financial plight was not the trade war in America, but the European war, which had dealt a heavy blow to British commerce. Napoleon had found himself unable to land his army in England, but he had other means of striking. In 1806 he issued the famous Berlin Decree, declaring that no other country should trade with his greatest enemy. Dealers had been wont to come every year to London from Germany, France, and Russia, in order to purchase the fine skins which the Hudson's Bay Company could supply. Now that this trade was lost to the company, the profits disappeared. For three seasons bale after bale of unsold peltry had been stacked to the rafters of the London warehouse.

The Earl of Selkirk was a practical man ; and, seeing the plight of the Hudson's Bay Company, he was tempted to take advantage of the situation to further his plans of emigration. Like a genuine lord of Galloway, however, he proceeded with extreme caution. His initial move was to get the best possible legal advice regarding the validity of the company's royal charter. Five of the foremost lawyers in the land were asked for their opinion upon this matter. Chief of those who were approached was Sir Samuel Romilly, the friend of Bentham and of Mirabeau. The other four were George Holroyd and James Scarlet, both distinguished pleaders, and William Cruise and John Bell. The finding of these lawyers put the question out of doubt. The charter, they said, was flawless. Of all the lands which were drained by the many rivers running into Hudson Bay, the company was the sole proprietor. Within these limits it could appoint sheriffs and bring law-breakers to trial. Besides, there was nothing to prevent it from granting to any one in fee-simple tracts of land in its vast domain.

Having satisfied himself that the charter of 1670 was legally unassailable, the earl was now ready for his subsequent line of action. He had resolved to get a foothold in the company itself. To effect this object he brought his own capital into play, and sought at the same time the aid of his wife's relatives, the Wedderburn-Colviles, and of other personal friends. Shares in the company had depreciated in value, and the owners, in many cases, were jubilant at the chance of getting them off their hands. Selkirk and his friends did not stop buying until they had acquired about one-third of the company's total stock.

In the meantime the Nor'westers scented trouble ahead. As soon as Lord Selkirk had completed his purchase of Hudson's Bay stock, he began to make overtures to the company's shareholders to be allowed to plant a colony in the territories assigned to them by their royal charter. To the Nor'-westers this proposition was anathema. They argued that if a permanent settlement was established in the fur country, the fur-bearing animals would be driven out, and their trade ruined. Their alarm grew apace. In May 1811 a general court of the Hudson's Bay Company, which had been adjourned, was on the point of reassembling. The London agents of the North-West Company decided to act at once. Forty-eight hours before the general court opened three of their number bought up a quantity of Hudson's Bay stock. One of these purchasers was the redoubtable explorer, Sir Alexander Mackenzie.

Straightway there ensued one of the liveliest sessions that ever occurred in a general court of the Hudson's Bay Company. The Nor'-

westers, who now had a right to voice their opinions, fumed and haggled. Other share holders flared into vigorous protest as the Earl of Selkirk's plan was disclosed. In the midst of the clash of interests, however, the earl's following stated his proposal succinctly. They said that Selkirk wished to secure a tract of fertile territory within the borders of Rupert's Land, for purposes of colonization. Preferably, this should lie in the region of the Red River, which ran northward towards Hudson Bay. At his own expense Selkirk would people this tract within a given period, foster the early efforts of its settlers, and appease the claims of the Indian tribes that inhabited the territory. He promised, moreover, to help to supply the Hudson's Bay Company with labourers for its work.

Had Lord Selkirk been present to view the animated throng of merchant adventurers, he would have foreseen his victory. In his first tilt with the Nor'westers he was to be successful. The opposition was strong, but it wore down before the onslaught of his friends. Then came the show of hands. There was no uncertainty about the vote : two - thirds of the court had pledged themselves in favour of Lord Selkirk's proposal.

By the terms of the grant which the general court made to Selkirk, he was to receive 116,000 square miles of virgin soil in the locality which he had selected. The boundaries of this immense area were carefully fixed. Roughly speaking, it extended from Big Island, in Lake Winnipeg, to the parting of the Red River from the head-waters of the Mississippi in the south, and from beyond the forks of the Red and Assiniboine rivers in the west to the shores of the Lake of the Woods, and at one point almost to Lake Superior, in the east. If a map is consulted, it will be seen that one-half of the grant lay in what is now the province of Manitoba, the other half in the present states of Minnesota and North Dakota.[1]

A great variety of opinions were expressed in London upon the subject of this grant. Some wiseacres said that the earl's proposal was as extravagant as it was visionary. One of Selkirk's acquaintances met him strolling along Pall Mall, and brought him up short on the street with the query : ' If you are bent

---

[1] It will be understood that the boundary-line between British and American territory in the North-West was not yet established. What afterwards became United States soil was at this time claimed by the Hudson's Bay Company under its charter.

on doing something futile, why do you not sow tares at home in order to reap wheat, or plough the desert of Sahara, which is nearer ? '

The extensive tract which the Hudson's Bay Company had bestowed upon Lord Selkirk for the nominal sum of ten shillings had made him the greatest individual land-owner in Christendom. His new possession was quite as large as the province of Egypt in the days of Caesar Augustus. But in some other respects Lord Selkirk's heritage was much greater. The province of Egypt, the granary of Rome, was fertile only along the banks of the Nile. More than three-fourths of Lord Selkirk's domain, on the other hand, was highly fertile soil.

CHAPTER IV

STORNOWAY—AND BEYOND

ON June 13, 1811, the deed was given to Selkirk of his wide possessions with the seal and signature of the Hudson's Bay Company, attached by Alexander Lean, the secretary. Before this, however, Selkirk had become deeply engrossed in the details of his enterprise. No time was to be lost, for unless all should be in readiness before the Hudson's Bay vessels set out to sea on their summer voyage, the proposed expedition of colonists must be postponed for another year.

Selkirk issued without delay a pamphlet, setting forth the advantages of the prospective colony. Land was to be given away free, or sold for a nominal sum. To the poor, transport would cost nothing ; others would have to pay according to their means. No one would be debarred on account of his religious belief ; all creeds were to be treated alike. The seat of the colony was to be called

Assiniboia, after a tribe of the Sioux nation, the Assiniboines, buffalo hunters on the Great Plains.

Wherever this pamphlet was read by men dissatisfied with their lot in the Old World, it aroused hope. With his usual good judgment, Selkirk had engaged several men whose training fitted them for the work of inducing landless men to emigrate. One of these was Captain Miles Macdonell, lately summoned by Lord Selkirk from his home in Canada. Macdonell had been reared in the Mohawk valley, had served in the ranks of the Royal Greens during the War of the Revolution, and had survived many a hard fight on the New York frontier. After the war, like most of his regiment, he had gone as a Loyalist to the county of Glengarry, on the Ottawa. It so chanced that the Earl of Selkirk while in Canada had met Macdonell, then a captain of the Royal Canadian Volunteers, and had been impressed by his courage and energy. In consequence, Selkirk now invited him to be the first governor of Assiniboia. Macdonell accepted the appointment; and promptly upon his arrival in Britain he went to the west coast of Ireland to win recruits for the settlement. Owing to the straitened circumstances of the Irish peasantry, the tide of emigration from Ireland was already running high, and Lord Selkirk thought that Captain Macdonell, who was a Roman Catholic, might influence some of his co-religionists to go to Assiniboia.

Another agent upon whom Selkirk felt that he could rely was Colin Robertson, a native of the island of Lewis, in the Hebrides. To this island he was now dispatched, with instructions to visit other sections of the Highlands as well. Robertson had formerly held a post under the North-West Company in the Saskatchewan valley. There he had quarrelled with a surly-natured trader known as Crooked-armed Macdonald, with the result that Robertson had been dismissed by the Nor'westers and had come back to Scotland in an angry mood.

A third place of muster for the colony was the city of Glasgow. There the Earl of Selkirk's representative was Captain Roderick M'Donald. Many Highlanders had gone to Glasgow, that busy hive of industry, in search of work. To the clerks in the shops and to the labourers in the yards or at the loom, M'Donald described the glories of Assiniboia. Many were impressed by his words, but objected to the low wages offered for their services. M'Donald compromised, and by offering a higher wage induced a number to enlist. But the recruits from Glasgow turned out to be a shiftless lot and a constant source of annoyance to Selkirk's officers.

While this work was being done the Nor'-westers in London were burning with wrath at their inability to hinder Lord Selkirk's project. Their hostility, we have seen, arose from their belief, which was quite correct, that a colony would interfere with their trading operations. In the hope that the enterprise might yet be stopped, they circulated in the Highlands various rumours against it. An anonymous attack, clearly from a Nor'wester source, appeared in the columns of the Inverness *Journal*. The author of this diatribe pictured the rigours of Assiniboia in terrible colours. Selkirk's agents were characterized as a brood of dissemblers. With respect to the earl himself words were not minced. His philanthropy was all assumed ; he was only biding his time in order to make large profits out of his colonization scheme.

Notwithstanding this campaign of slander, groups of would-be settlers came straggling along from various places to the port of rendezvous, Stornoway, the capital of the

Hebrides. When all had gathered, these
people who had answered the call to a new
heritage beyond the seas proved to be a motley
throng.   Some were stalwart men in the prime
of life, men who looked forward to homes of
their own on a distant shore ;   others, with
youth on their side, were eager for the trail
of the flying moose or the sight of a painted
redskin ;   a few were women, steeled to
bravery through fires of want and sorrow.
Too many were wastrels, cutting adrift from
a blighted past.   A goodly number were mal-
contents, wondering whether to go or stay.

The leading vessel of the Hudson's Bay
fleet in the year 1811 was the commodore's
ship, the *Prince of Wales*.   At her moorings
in the Thames another ship, the *Eddystone*,
lay ready for the long passage to the Great
Bay.   Besides these, a shaky old hulk, the
Edward and Ann, was put into commission for
the use of Lord Selkirk's settlers.   Her grey
sails were mottled with age and her rigging
was loose and worn.   Sixteen men and boys
made up her crew, a number by no means
sufficient for a boat of her size.   It seemed
almost criminal to send such an ill-manned
craft out on the tempestuous North Atlantic.
However, the three ships sailed from the

Thames and steered up the east coast of England. Opposite Yarmouth a gale rose and forced them into a sheltering harbour. It was the middle of July before they rounded the north shore of Scotland. At Stromness in the Orkneys the *Prince of Wales* took on board a small body of emigrants and a number of the company's servants who were waiting there.

At length the tiny fleet reached the bustling harbour-town of Stornoway ; and here Miles Macdonell faced a task of no little difficulty. Counting the Orkneymen just arrived, there were one hundred and twenty-five in his party. The atmosphere seemed full of unrest, and the cause was not far to seek. The Nor'westers were at work, and their agents were sowing discontent among the emigrants. Even Collector Reed, the government official in charge of the customs, was acting as the tool of the Nor'westers. It was Reed's duty, of course, to hasten the departure of the expedition ; but instead of doing this he put every possible obstacle in the way. Moreover, he mingled with the emigrants, urging them to forsake the venture while there was yet time.

Another partisan of the North-West Company also appeared on the scene. This was an army officer named Captain Mackenzie, who pretended to be gathering recruits for the army. He had succeeded, it appears, in getting some of Selkirk's men to take the king's shilling, and now was trying to lead these men away from the ships as ' deserters from His Majesty's service.' One day this trouble-maker brought his dinghy alongside one of the vessels. A sailor on deck, who saw Captain Mackenzie in the boat and was eager for a lark, picked up a nine-pound shot, poised it carefully, and let it fall. There was a splintering thud. Captain Mackenzie suddenly remembered how dry it was on shore, and put off for land as fast as oars would hurry him. Next day he sent a pompous challenge to the commander of the vessel. It was, of course, ignored.

In spite of obstacles, little by little the arrangements for the ocean voyage were being completed. There were many irritating delays. Disputes about wages broke out afresh when inequalities were discovered. There was much wrangling among the emigrants as to their quarters on the uninviting *Edward and Ann*. At the last moment a number of the party took fear and decided to stay at home.

Some left the ship in unceremonious fashion, even forgetting their effects. These were subsequently sold among the passengers. 'One man,' wrote Captain Macdonell, 'jumped into the sea and swam for it until he was picked up.' It may be believed that the governor of Assiniboia heaved a thankful sigh when the ships were ready to hoist their sails. 'It has been a herculean task,' ran the text of his parting message to the Earl of Selkirk.

On July 26 a favourable breeze bore the vessels out to sea. There were now one hundred and five in the party, seventy of whom had professed an intention to till the soil. The remainder had been indentured as servants of the Hudson's Bay Company. Seventy-six of the total number were quartered on board the *Edward and Ann*. As the vessels swept seaward many eyes were fastened sadly on the receding shore. The white houses of Stornoway loomed up distinctly across the dark waters of the bay. The hill which rose gloomily in the background was treeless and inky black. On the clean shingle lay the cod and herring, piled loose to catch the sun's warm rays. The settlers remembered that they were perhaps scanning for the last time the rugged outline of that heather-clad landscape, and their hearts grew sick within them. Foreland after foreland came into view and disappeared. At length the ships were skirting the Butt of Lewis with its wave-worn clefts and caverns. Then all sight of land vanished, and they were steering their course into the northern main.

A man-of-war had been sent as a convoy to the vessels, for the quick-sailing frigates of France had been harrying British shipping, and the mercantile marine needed protection. After standing guard to a point four hundred miles off the Irish coast, the ship-of-the-line turned back, and the three vessels held their way alone in a turbulent sea. Two of them beat stoutly against the gale, but the *Edward and Ann* hove to for a time, her timbers creaking and her bowsprit catching the water as she rose and fell with the waves. And so they put out into the wide and wild Atlantic—these poor, homeless, storm-tossed exiles, who were to add a new chapter to Great Britain's colonial history.

CHAPTER V

WINTERING ON THE BAY

LITTLE is known of the many strange things which must have taken place on the voyage. On board the *Edward and Ann* sickness was prevalent and the ship's surgeon was kept busy. There were few days on which the passengers could come from below-decks. When weather permitted, Captain Macdonell, who knew the dangers to be encountered in the country they were going to, attempted to give the emigrants military drill. ' There never was a more awkward squad,' was his opinion, ' not a man, or even officer, of the party knew how to put a gun to his eye or had ever fired a shot.' A prominent figure on the *Edward and Ann* was a careless-hearted cleric, whose wit and banter were in evidence throughout the voyage. This was the Reverend Father Burke, an Irish priest. He had stolen away without the leave of his bishop, and it appears that he and Macdonell,

although of the same faith, were not the best
of friends.

After a stormy voyage of nearly two months
the ships entered the long, barren straits leading into Hudson Bay. From the beginning of
September the fleet had been hourly expected
at York Factory, and speculation was rife
there as to its delay in arriving. On September 24 the suspense ended, for the look-out
at the fort descried the ships moving in from
the north and east. They anchored in the
shallow haven on the western shore, where
two streams, the Nelson and the Hayes, enter
Hudson Bay, and the sorely tried passengers
disembarked. They were at once marched
to York Factory, on the north bank of the
Hayes. The strong palisades and wooden
bastions of the fort warned the newcomers
that there were dangers in America to be
guarded against. A pack of ' husky ' dogs
came bounding forth to meet them as they
approached the gates.

A survey of the company's buildings convinced Macdonell that much more roomy
quarters would be required for the approaching winter, and he determined to erect suitable habitations for his people before snowfall.
With this in view he crossed over to the Nelson

and ascended it until he reached a high clearing on its left bank, near which grew an abundance of white spruce. He brought up a body of men, most of whom now received their first lesson in woodcraft. The pale and flaky-barked aromatic spruce trees were felled and stripped of their branches. Next, the logs were ' snaked ' into the open, where the dwellings were to be erected, and hewed into proper shape. These timbers were then deftly fitted together and the four walls of a rude but substantial building began to rise. A drooping roof was added, the chinks were closed, and then the structure was complete. When a sufficient number of such houses had been built, Macdonell set the party to work cutting firewood and gathering it into convenient piles.

The prudence of these measures became apparent when the frost king fixed his iron grip upon land and sea. As the days shortened, the rivers were locked deep and fast ; a sharp wind penetrated the forest, and the salty bay was fringed with jagged and glistening hummocks of ice. So severe was the cold that the newcomers were loath to go forth from their warm shelter even to haul food from the fort over the brittle, yielding snow. Under such conditions life in the camp grew monotonous and dull. More serious still, the food they had to eat was the common fare of such isolated winterers ; it was chiefly salt meat. The effect of this was seen as early as December. Some of the party became listless and sluggish, their faces turned sallow and their eyes appeared sunken. They found it difficult to breathe and their gums were swollen and spongy. Macdonell, a veteran in hardship, saw at once that scurvy had broken out among them ; but he had a simple remedy and the supply was without limit. The sap of the white spruce was extracted and administered to the sufferers. Almost immediately their health showed improvement, and soon all were on the road to recovery. But the medicine was not pleasant to take, and some of the party at first foolishly refused to submit to the treatment.

The settlers, almost unwittingly, banded together into distinct groups, each individual tending to associate with the others from his own home district. As time went on these groups, with their separate grievances, gave Macdonell much trouble. The Orkneymen, who were largely servants of the Hudson's Bay Company, were not long in incurring his disfavour.   To him they seemed to have the appetites of a pack of hungry wolves.   He dubbed them ' lazy, spiritless and ill-disposed.' The ' Glasgow rascals,' too, were a source of annoyance.   'A more ... cross-grained lot,' he asserted, ' were never put under any person's care.'

Owing to the discord existing in the camp, the New Year was not ushered in happily. In Scotland, of all the days of the year, this anniversary was held in the highest regard. It was generally celebrated to the strains of ' Weel may we a' be,' and with effusive hand-shakings, much dining, and a hot kettle.   The lads from the Orkneys were quite wide awake to the occasion and had no intention of omitting the customs of their sires.   On New Year's Day they were having a rollicking time in one of the cabins.   But their enthusiasm was quickly damped by a party of Irish who, having primed their courage with whisky, set upon the merry-makers and created a scene of wild disorder.   In the heat of the *mêlée* three of the Orkneymen were badly beaten, and for a month their lives hung in the balance.   Captain Macdonell later sent several of the Irish back to Great Britain, saying that such ' worthless blackguards ' were

THE COUNTRY OF
LORD SELKIRK'S
SETTLERS

Bartholomew, Edin.

better under the discipline of the army or the navy.

One of the number who had not taken kindly to Miles Macdonell as a ' medicine-man ' was William Findlay, a very obdurate Orkneyman, who had flatly refused to soil his lips with the wonder-working syrup of the white spruce. Shortly afterwards, having been told to do something, he was again dis-obedient. This time he was forced to appear before Magistrate Hillier of the Hudson's Bay Company and was condemned to gaol. As there was really no such place, a log-house was built for Findlay, and he was imprisoned in it. A gruff-noted babel of dissent arose among his kinsfolk, supported by the men from Glasgow. A gang of thirteen, in which both parties were represented, put a match to the prison where Findlay was confined, and rescued its solitary inmate out of the blaze. Then, uttering defiance, they seized another building, and decided to live apart. Thus, with the attitude of rebels and well supplied with firearms, they kept the rest of the camp in a state of nervousness for several months. In June, however, these rebels allowed them-selves to fall into a trap. Having crossed the Nelson, they found their return cut off by the melting of the ice. This put them at the mercy of the officials at York Factory, and they were forced to surrender. After receiving their humble acknowledgments Macdonell was not disposed to treat them severely, and he took them back into service.

But what of jovial Father Burke since his arrival on the shores of Hudson Bay ? To all appearances, he had not been able to restrain his flock from mischief. He had, however, been exploring on his own account, and thoroughly believed that he had made some valuable discoveries. He had come upon pebbles of various kinds which he thought were precious stones. Some of them shone like diamonds ; others seemed like rubies. Father Burke was indeed sure that bits of the sand which he had collected contained particles of gold. Macdonell himself believed that the soil along the Nelson abounded in mineral wealth. He told the priest to keep the discovery a secret, and sent samples of sand and stone to Lord Selkirk, advising him to acquire the banks of the Nelson river from the company. In the end, to the disgust of Macdonell and Father Burke, not one sample proved of any value.

Weeks before the ice had left the river, the

colonists became impatient to set forward on the remainder of their journey. To transport so many persons, with all their belongings and with sufficient provisions, seven or eight hundred miles inland was an undertaking formidable enough to put Captain Macdonell's energies to the fullest test. The only craft available were bark canoes, and these would be too fragile for the heavy cargoes that must be borne. Stouter boats must be built. Macdonell devised a sort of punt or flat-bottomed boat, such as he had formerly seen in the colony of New York. Four of these clumsy craft were constructed, but only with great difficulty, and after much trouble with the workmen. Inefficiency, as well as misconduct, on the part of the colonists was a sore trial to Macdonell. The men from the Hebrides were now practically the only members of the party who were not, for one reason or another, in his black book.

It was almost midsummer before the boats began to push up the Hayes river for the interior. There were many blistered hands at the oars; nevertheless, on the journey they managed to make an average of thirteen miles each day. Before the colonists could reach Oxford House, the next post of the Hudson's

Bay Company, three dozen portages had to be passed. It was with thankful hearts that they came to Holy Lake and caught sight of the trading-post by its margin. Here was an ample reach of water, reminding the Highlanders of a loch of far-away Scotland. When the wind died down, Holy Lake was like a giant mirror. Looking into its quiet waters, the voyagers saw great fish swimming swiftly.

From Oxford House the route lay over a height-of-land to the head-waters of the Nelson. After a series of difficulties the party reached Norway House, another post of the Hudson's Bay Company, on an upper arm of Lake Winnipeg. At this time Norway House was the centre of the great fur-bearing region. The colonists found it strongly entrenched in a rocky basin and astir with life. After a short rest they proceeded towards Lake Winnipeg, and soon were moving slowly down its low-lying eastern shore. Here they had their first glimpse of the prairie country, with its green carpet of grass. Out from the water's edge grew tall, lank reeds, the lurking place of snipe and sand-piper. Doubtless, in the brief night-watches, they listened to the shrill cry of the restless lynx, or heard the yapping howl of the timber wolf as he slunk

away among the copses. But presently the
boats were gliding in through the sand-choked
outlet of the Red River, and they were on the
last stage of their journey.

Some forty miles up-stream from its mouth
the Red River bends sharply towards the east,
forming what is known as Point Douglas in
the present city of Winnipeg. Having toiled
round this point, the colonists pushed their
boats to the muddy shore. The day they
landed—the natal day of a community which
was to grow into three great provinces of
Canada—was August 30, 1812.

CHAPTER VI

RED RIVER AND PEMBINA

SCARCELY had the settlers taken stock of their surroundings on the Red River when they were chilled to the marrow with a sudden terror. Towards them came racing on horseback a formidable-looking troop, decked out in all the accoutrements of the Indian—spreading feather, dangling tomahawk, and a thick coat of war-paint. To the newcomers it was a never-to-be-forgotten spectacle. But when the riders came within close range, shouting and gesticulating, it was seen that they wore borrowed apparel, and that their speech was a medley of French and Indian dialects. They were a troop of Bois Brûlés, Métis, or half-breeds of French and Indian blood, aping for the time the manners of their mothers' people. Their object was to tell Lord Selkirk's party that settlers were not wanted on the Red River ; that it was the country of the fur traders, and that settlers must go farther afield.

This was surely an inhospitable reception, after a long and fatiguing journey. Plainly the Nor'westers were at it again, trying now to frighten the colonists away, as they had tried before to keep them from coming. These mounted half-breeds were a deputation from Fort Gibraltar, the Nor'westers' nearest trading-post, which stood two miles higher up at ' the Forks,' where the Red River is joined by the Assiniboine.

Nevertheless, Governor Macdonell, having planned as dignified a ceremony as the circumstances would allow, sent to the Nor'westers at Fort Gibraltar an invitation to be present at the official inauguration of Lord Selkirk's colony. At the appointed hour, on September 4, several traders from the fort, together with a few French Canadians and Indians, put in an appearance. In the presence of this odd company Governor Macdonell read the Earl of Selkirk's patent to Assiniboia. About him was drawn up a guard of honour, and overhead the British ensign fluttered in the breeze. Six small swivel-guns, which had been brought with the colonists, belched forth a salute to mark the occasion. The Nor'westers were visibly impressed by this show of authority and power. In pretended friendship they entered Governor Macdonell's tent and accepted his hospitality before departing. At variance with the scowls of trapper and trader towards the settlers was the attitude of the full-blooded Indians who were camping along the Red River. From the outset these redskins were friendly, and their conduct was soon to stand the settlers in good stead.

The provisions brought from Hudson Bay were fast diminishing and would soon be at an end. True, the Nor'westers offered for sale supplies of oats, barley, poultry, and the like, but their prices were high and the settlers had not the means of purchase. But there was other food. Myriads of buffalo roamed over the Great Plains. Herds of these animals often darkened the horizon like a slowly moving cloud. In summer they might be seen cropping the prairie grass, or plunging and rolling about in muddy ' wallows.' In winter they moved to higher levels, where lay less snow to be removed from the dried grass which they devoured. At that season those who needed to hunt the buffalo for food must follow them wherever they went. This was now the plight of the settlers : winter was coming on and food was already scarce. The settlers must seek out the winter haunts of the buffalo.

The Indians were of great service, for they offered to act as guides.

A party to hunt the buffalo was organized. Like a train of pilgrims, the majority of the colonists now set out afoot. Their dark-skinned escort, mounted on wiry ponies, bent their course in a southerly direction. The redskins eyed with amusement the queer-clad strangers whom they were guiding. These were ignorant of the ways of the wild prairie country and badly equipped to face its difficulties. Sometimes the Indians indulged in horse-play, and a few of them were unable to keep their hands off the settlers' possessions. One Highlander lost an ancient musket which he treasured. A wedding ring was taken by an Indian guide from the hand of one of the women. Five days of straggling march brought the party to a wide plateau where the Indians said that the buffalo were accustomed to pasture. Here the party halted, at the junction of the Red and Pembina rivers, and awaited the arrival of Captain Macdonell, who came up next day on horseback with three others of his party.

Temporary tents and cabins were erected, and steps were taken to provide more commodious shelters. But this second winter threatened to be almost as uncomfortable as the first had been on Hudson Bay.   Captain Macdonell selected a suitable place south of the Pembina river, and on this site a storehouse and other buildings were put up.   The end of the year saw a neat little encampment, surrounded by palisades, where before had been nothing but unbroken prairie.   As a finishing touch, a flagstaff was raised within the stockade, and in honour of one of Lord Selkirk's titles the name Fort Daer was given to the whole.   In the meantime a body of seventeen Irishmen, led by Owen Keveny, had arrived from the old country, having accomplished the feat of making their way across the ocean to Hudson Bay and up to the settlement during the single season of 1812.   This additional force was housed at once in Fort Daer along with the rest.   Until spring opened, buffalo meat was to be had in plenty, the Indians bringing in quantities of it for a slight reward.   So unconscious were the buffalo of danger that they came up to the very palisades, giving the settlers an excellent view of their drab-brown backs and fluffy, curling manes.

On the departure of the herds in the springtime there was no reason why the colonists

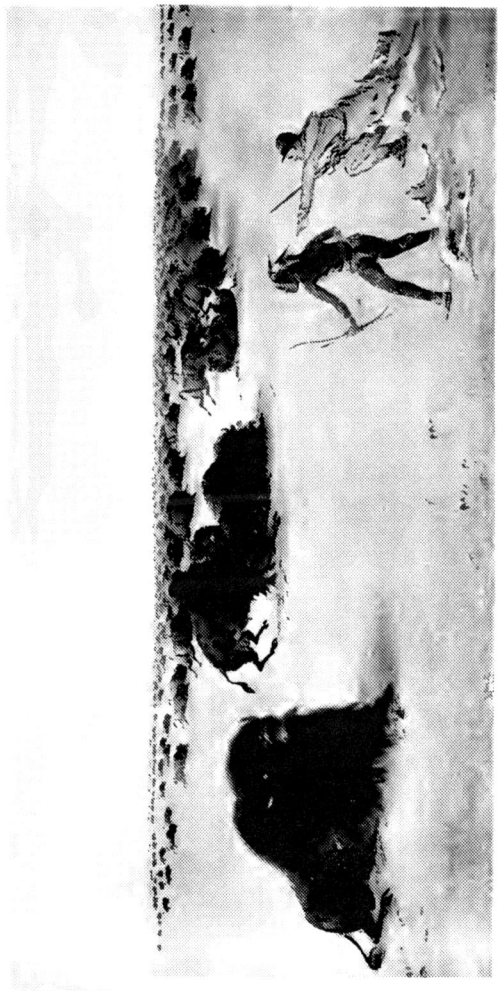

HUNTING THE BUFFALO
From a painting by George Catlin

should remain any longer at Fort Daer. Accordingly the entire band plodded wearily back to the ground which they had vacated above 'the Forks' on the Red River. As the season of 1813 advanced, more solid structures were erected on this site, and the place became known as Colony Gardens. An attempt was now made to prepare the soil and to sow some seed, but it was a difficult task, as the only agricultural implement possessed by the settlers was the hoe. They next turned to the river in search of food, only to find it almost empty of fish. Even the bushes, upon which clusters of wild berries ought to have been found, were practically devoid of fruit. Nature seemed to have veiled her countenance from the hapless settlers, and to be mocking their most steadfast efforts. In their dire need they were driven to use weeds for food. An indigenous plant called the prairie apple grew in abundance, and the leaves of a species of the goosefoot family were found to be nourishing.

With the coming of autumn 1813 the experiences of the previous year were repeated. Once more they went over the dreary road to Fort Daer. Then followed the most cruel winter that the settlers had yet endured. The snow fell thickly and lay in heavy drifts, and the buffalo with animal foresight had wandered to other fields. The Nor'westers sold the colonists a few provisions, but were egging on their allies, the Bois Brûlés, who occupied a small post in the vicinity of the Pembina, to annoy them whenever possible. It required courage of the highest order on the part of the colonists to battle through the winter. They were in extreme poverty, and in many cases their frost-bitten, starved bodies were wrapped only in rags before spring came. Those who still had their plaids, or other presentable garments, were prepared to part with them for a morsel of food. With the coming of spring once more, the party travelled north-ward to ' the Forks ' of the Red River, re-solved never again to set foot within the gates of Fort Daer.

Meanwhile, some news of the desperate state of affairs on the Red River had reached the Earl of Selkirk in Scotland. So many were the discouragements that one might for-give him if at this juncture he had flung his colonizing scheme to the winds as a lost ven-ture. The lord of St Mary's Isle did not, however, abandon hope ; he was a persistent man and not easily turned aside from his purpose. Now he went in person to the straths and glens of Sutherlandshire to recruit more settlers. For several years the crofters in this section of the Highlands had been ejected in ruthless fashion from their holdings. Those who aimed to ' quench the smoke of cottage fires ' had sent a regiment of soldiers into this shire to cow the Highlanders into submission. Lord Selkirk came at a critical moment and extended a helping hand to the outcasts. A large company agreed to join the colony of Assiniboia, and under Selkirk's own superintendence they were equipped for the journey. As the sad-eyed exiles were about to leave the port of Helmsdale, the earl passed among them, dispensing words of comfort and of cheer.

This contingent numbered ninety-seven persons. The vessel carrying them from Helmsdale reached the *Prince of Wales* of the Hudson's Bay Company, on which they embarked, at Stromness in the Orkneys. The parish of Kildonan, in Sutherlandshire, had the largest representation among these emigrants. Names commonly met with on the ship's register were Gunn, Matheson, MacBeth, Sutherland, and Bannerman.

After the *Prince of Wales* had put to sea,

fever broke out on board, and the contagion quickly spread among the passengers. Many of them died. They had escaped from beggary on shore only to perish at sea and to be consigned to a watery grave. The vessel reached Hudson Bay in good time, but for some unknown reason the captain put into Churchill, over a hundred miles north of York Factory. This meant that the newcomers must camp on the Churchill for the winter ; there was nothing else to be done. Fortunately partridge were numerous in the neighbourhood of their encampment, and, as the uneventful months dragged by, the settlers had an unstinted supply of fresh food. In April 1814 forty-one members of the party, about half of whom were women, undertook to walk over the snow to York Factory. The men drew the sledges on which their provisions were loaded and went in advance, clearing the way for the women. In the midst of the company strode a solemn-visaged piper. At one moment, as a dirge wailed forth, the spirits of the people drooped and they felt themselves beaten and forsaken. But anon the music changed. Up through the scrubby pine and over the mantle of snow rang the skirl of the undefeated ; and as they heard the gathering song of Bonnie Dundee or the summons to fight for Royal Charlie, they pressed forward with unfaltering steps.

This advance party came to York Factory, and, continuing the journey, reached Colony Gardens without misadventure early in the summer. They were better husbandmen than their predecessors, and they quickly addressed themselves to the cultivation of the soil. Thirty or forty bushels of potatoes were planted in the black loam of the prairie. These yielded a substantial increase. The thrifty Sutherlanders might have saved the tottering colony, had not Governor Macdonell committed an act which, however legally right, was nothing less than foolhardy in the circumstances, and which brought disaster in its train.

In his administration of the affairs of the colony Macdonell had shown good executive ability and a willingness to endure every trial that his followers endured. Towards the Nor'westers, however, he was inclined to be stubborn and arrogant. He was convinced that he must adopt stringent measures against them. He determined to assert his authority as governor of the colony under Lord Selkirk's patent. Undoubtedly Macdonell had reason to be indignant at the unfriendly attitude of the fur traders; yet, so far, this had merely taken the form of petty annoyance, and might have been met by good nature and diplomacy.

In January 1814 Governor Macdonell issued a proclamation pronouncing it unlawful for any person who dealt in furs to remove from the colony of Assiniboia supplies of flesh, fish, grain, or vegetable. Punishment would be meted out to those who offended against this official order. The aim of Macdonell was to keep a supply of food in the colony for the support of the new settlers. He was, however, offering a challenge to the fur traders, for his policy meant in effect that these had no right in Assiniboia, that it was to be kept for the use of settlers alone. Such a mandate could not fail to rouse intense hostility among the traders, whose doctrine was the very opposite. The Nor'westers were quick to seize the occasion to strike at the struggling colony.

N

PLAN OF
RED RIVER COLONY

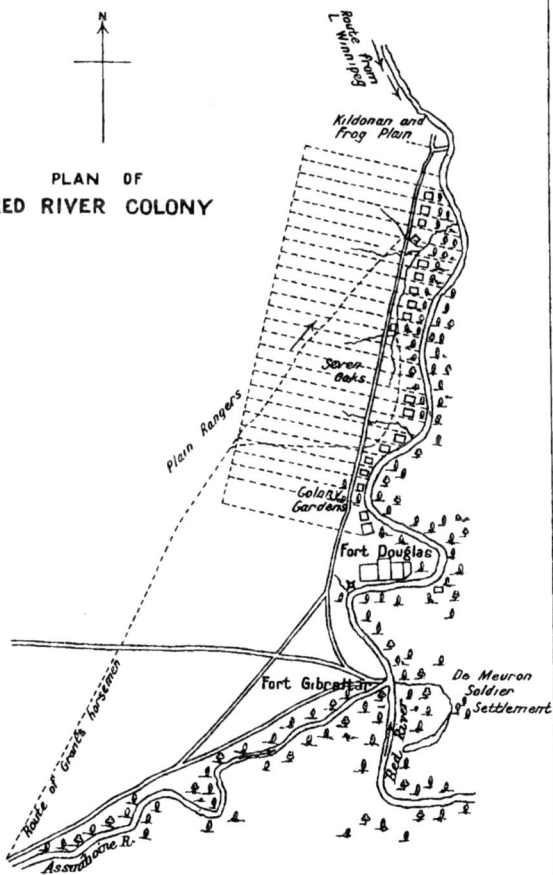

Route from
L. Winnipeg

Kildonan and
Frog Plain

Seven
Oaks

Plain Rangers

Colony
Gardens

Fort Douglas

Fort Gibraltar

De Meuron
Soldier
Settlement

Red River

Route of Grant's horsemen

Assiniboine R.

Edin'

CHAPTER VII

THE BEGINNING OF STRIFE

STORMY days were coming. Once Governor Macdonell had published his edict, he did not hesitate to enforce its terms. Information had been received at Colony Gardens that the Nor'westers had stored a quantity of provisions in their trading-post at the mouth of the Souris, a large southern tributary of the Assiniboine. It was clear that, in defiance of Macdonell's decree, they meant to send food supplies out of Assiniboia to support their trading-posts elsewhere. The fort at Souris was in close proximity to Brandon House on the Assiniboine, a post founded by the Hudson's Bay Company in 1794. Macdonell decided on strong action. His secretary, John Spencer, was ordered to go to the Souris in the capacity of a sheriff, accompanied by a strong guard and carrying a warrant in his pocket. When Spencer drew near the stockades of the Nor'westers' fort and found the gate closed against him, he commanded his men to batter it in with their hatchets. They obeyed with alacrity, and having filed inside the fort, took charge of the contents of the storehouse. Six hundred bags of pemmican were seized and carried to Brandon House. Already there was a state of war in Assiniboia.

The territory which comprised the colony was of great value economically to the North-West Company. The food supplies which supported its traders in the far interior were largely drawn from this area. In the eyes of the Nor'westers, Sheriff John Spencer had performed an act of pure brigandage at their Souris post. Still, they were in no hurry to execute a counter-move. In order to make no mistake they thought it best to restrain themselves until their partners should hold their summer meeting at Fort William,[1] on Lake Superior.

The partners of the North-West Company

---

[1] After it had been discovered that the Grand Portage was situated partly on land awarded by treaty to the United States, the Nor'westers, in 1803, had erected a new factory thirty or forty miles farther north where the Kaministikwia river enters Thunder Bay. This post became their chief fur emporium west of Montreal, and was given the name Fort William as a tribute to William M'Gillivray, one of the leading partners in the company.

met at Fort William in the month of July
1814. Their fond hope had been that Lord
Selkirk's colony would languish and die.
Instead, it was flourishing and waxing aggressive. The governor of Assiniboia had published an edict which he seemed determined
to enforce, to the ruin of the business of the
North-West Company. The grizzled partners,
as they rubbed elbows in secret conclave,
decided that something must be done to crush
this troublesome settlement. Whether or not
they formed any definite plan cannot be
ascertained. It is scarcely believable that at
this meeting was plotted the opposition to
Lord Selkirk's enterprise which was to begin
with deceit and perfidy and to culminate in
bloodshed. Among the Nor'westers were men
of great worth and integrity. There were,
however, others in their ranks who proved
base and irresponsible. During this confer-
ence at Fort William a bitter animosity was
expressed against Lord Selkirk and the company which had endorsed his colonizing
project. It was the Nor'westers' misfortune
and fault that some of their number were prepared to vent this outspoken enmity in deeds
of criminal violence.

Two 'wintering partners' of the North-

West Company—men who remained in the
interior during the winter—appear to have
been entrusted by their fellows with the task
of dealing with the settlers on the Red River.
Both these men, Duncan Cameron and Alexander Macdonell, had a wide experience of the
prairie country.   Of the pair, Cameron was
unquestionably the more resourceful.   In view
of the fact that later in life he became a trusted
representative of the county of Glengarry in
the legislature of Upper Canada, there has
been a tendency to gloss over some of his mis-
demeanours when he was still a trader in furs.
But he was a sinister character.   His principal
aim, on going to the Red River, was to pay
lavish court to the settlers in order to de-
ceive them.   He was a born actor, and could
assume at will the gravest or the gayest of
demeanours or any disposition he chose to
put on.

Alexander Macdonell, the other emissary of
the Nor'westers, was of an inferior type.   He
was crafty enough never to burn his own
fingers.   Macdonell had some influence over
the Indians of the Qu'Appelle district and of
the more distant west.   His immediate proposal was to attract a band of redskins to the
neighbourhood of Colony Gardens with the

avowed intention of creating a panic among the settlers.

Shortly after the July meeting at Fort William these two men started on their mission for the Red River. On August 5, while at a stopping-point by the way, Alexander Macdonell dated a letter to a friend in Montreal. The tenor of this letter would indicate that only a portion of the Nor'westers were ready to adopt extreme measures against the settlement. 'Something serious will undoubtedly take place,' was Macdonell's callous admission. 'Nothing but the complete downfall of the colony,' he continued, 'will satisfy some, by fair or foul means—a most desirable object if it can be accomplished. So here is at them with all my heart and energy.'

Towards the end of August the twain arrived at Fort Gibraltar, where they parted company. Alexander Macdonell proceeded to his winter quarters at Fort Qu'Appelle, on the river of the same name which empties into the upper Assiniboine. Duncan Cameron made his appearance with considerable pomp and circumstance at Fort Gibraltar. The settlers soon knew him as 'Captain' Duncan Cameron, of the Voyageur Corps, a battalion which had ranged the border during the recent war with the United States. Cameron decked himself in a crimson uniform. He had a sword by his side and the outward bearing of a gallant officer. Lest there should be any want of belief on the part of the colonists, he caused his credentials to be tacked up on the gateway of Fort Gibraltar. There, in legible scrawl, was an order appointing him as captain and Alexander Macdonell as lieutenant in the Voyageur Corps. The sight of a soldier sent a thrill through the breasts of the Highlanders and the fight-loving Irish. Cameron had in fact once belonged to the Voyageurs, and no one at Colony Gardens yet knew that the corps had been disbanded the year before. At a later date Lord Selkirk took pains to prove that Cameron had been guilty of rank imposture.

To pose in the guise of a captain of militia was not Duncan Cameron's only rôle. Having impressed his martial importance upon all, he next went among the settlers as a comrade. He could chat at ease in Gaelic, and this won the confidence of the Highlanders. Some of the colonists were invited to his table. These he treated with studied kindness, and he furnished them with such an abundance of good food that they felt disgust for the scant

and humble fare allowed them at the settlement.   At the same time Cameron began to
make bold insinuations in his conversation.
He had, he said, heard news from the interior
that a body of Indians would raid them in the
spring.   He harped upon the deplorable state
in which the settlers were living ; out of fellow-
feeling for them, he said, he would gladly act
as their deliverer.   Why did they not throw
themselves upon the mercies of the North-
West Company ?   In their unhappy condition,
abandoned, as he hinted, by Lord Selkirk to
their own resources, there was but one thing
for them to do.   They must leave the Red
River far behind, and he would guarantee
that the Nor'westers would assist them.

As a result of Cameron's intrigues, signs of
wavering allegiance were soon in evidence.
One of the settlers in particular, George
Campbell, became a traitor in the camp.
Campbell had negotiated with Lord Selkirk
personally during Selkirk's visit to Sutherlandshire.   Now he complained vigorously of his
treatment since leaving Scotland, and was in
favour of accepting the terms which Cameron,
as a partner in the North-West Company,
offered.   As many colonists as desired it, said
Cameron, would be transported by the Nor'-

westers free of charge to Montreal or other parts of Canada. A year's provisions would be supplied to them, and each colonist would be granted two hundred acres of fertile land. Tempting bribes of money were offered some of them as a bait. An influential Highlander, Alexander M'Lean, was promised two hundred pounds from Cameron's own pocket, on condition that he would take his family away. Several letters which were penned by the sham officer during the winter of 1815 can still be read. ' I am glad,' he wrote to a couple of settlers in February, ' that the eyes of some of you are getting open at last . . . and that you now see your past follies in obeying the unlawful orders of a plunderer, and I may say, of a highway robber, for what took place here last spring can be called nothing else but manifest robbery.'

As yet Duncan Cameron had refrained from the use of force, but as winter wore on towards spring he saw that, to complete his work, force would be necessary. The proportion of settlers remaining loyal to Lord Selkirk was by no means insignificant, and Cameron feared the pieces of artillery at Colony Gardens. He decided on a bold effort to get these field-pieces into his possession.

Early in April he made a startling move. Miles Macdonell was away at Fort Daer, and Archibald Macdonald, the deputy-governor of the colony, was in charge. To him Cameron sent a peremptory demand in writing for the field-pieces, that they might be ' out of harm's way.'

This missive was first given into the hands of the traitor George Campbell, who read it to the settlers on Sunday after church. Next day, while rations were being distributed, it was delivered to the deputy-governor in the colony storehouse. About one o'clock on the same afternoon, George Campbell and a few kindred spirits broke into the building where the field-pieces were stored, took the guns outside, and placed them on horse-sledges for the purpose of drawing them away. At this juncture a musket was fired as a signal, and Duncan Cameron with some Bois Brûlés stole from a clump of trees. ' Well done, my hearty fellows,' Cameron exclaimed, as he came hurrying up. The guns were borne away and lodged within the precincts of Fort Gibraltar, and a number of the colonists now took sides openly with Duncan Cameron and the Nor'westers.

Meanwhile Cameron's colleague, Alexander

Macdonell, was not succeeding in his efforts to incite the Indians about Fort Qu'Appelle against the colony. He found that the Indians did not lust for the blood of the settlers; and when he appeared at Fort Gibraltar, in May, he had with him only a handful of Plain Crees. These redskins lingered about the fort for a time, being well supplied with liquor to make them pot-valiant. During their stay a number of horses belonging to the settlers were wounded by arrows, but it is doubtful if the perpetrators of these outrages were Indians. The chief of the Crees finally visited Governor Miles Macdonell, and convinced him that his warriors intended the colonists no ill. Before the Indians departed they sent to Colony Gardens a pipe of peace— the red man's token of friendship.

An equally futile attempt was made about the same time by two traders of the North-West Company to persuade Katawabetay, chief of the Chippewas, to lead a band of his tribesmen against the settlement. Katawabetay was at Sand Lake, just west of Lake Superior, when his parley with the Nor'westers took place. The two traders promised to give Katawabetay and his warriors all the merchandise and rum in three of the company's posts, if they would raise the hatchet and descend upon the Red River settlers. The cautious chief wished to know whether this was the desire of the military authorities. The traders had to confess that it was merely a wish of the North-West Company. Katawabetay then demurred, saying that, before beginning hostilities, he must speak about the matter to one of the provincial military leaders on St Joseph's Island, at the head of Lake Huron.

Finding it impossible to get the Indians to raid the settlement, Cameron now adopted other methods. His party had been increasing in numbers day by day. Joined by the deserters from the colony, the Nor'westers pitched their camp a short distance down the river from Fort Gibraltar. At this point guns were mounted, and at Fort Gibraltar Cameron's men were being drilled. On June 11 a chosen company, furnished with loaded muskets and ammunition, were marched towards Governor Macdonell's house, where they concealed themselves behind some trees. James White, the surgeon of the colony, was seen walking close to the house. A puff of grey smoke came from the Nor'westers' cover. The shot went wide. Then John Bourke, the store-keeper, heard a bullet whiz by his head, and narrowly escaped death. The colonists at once seized their arms and answered the Nor'westers' fire. In the exchange of volleys, however, they were at a disadvantage, as their adversaries remained hidden from view. When the Nor'westers decamped, four persons on the colonists' side had been wounded.

Apparently there was no longer security for life or property among those still adhering to Lord Selkirk's cause at Colony Gardens. Duncan Cameron, employing a subterfuge, now said that his main object was to capture Governor Macdonell. If this were accomplished he would leave the settlers unmolested. In order to safeguard the colony Macdonell voluntarily surrendered himself to the Nor'-westers. Cameron was jubilant. With the loyal settlers worsted and almost defenceless, and the governor of Assiniboia his prisoner, he could dictate his own terms. He issued an explicit command that the settlers must vacate the Red River without delay. A majority of the settlers decided to obey, and their exodus began under Cameron's guidance. About one hundred and forty, inclusive of women and children, stepped into the canoes of the North-West Company to be borne away to Canada. Miles Macdonell was taken to Montreal under arrest.

The forty or fifty colonists who still clung to their homes at Colony Gardens were left to be dealt with by Alexander Macdonell, who was nothing loath to finish Cameron's work of destruction. Once more muskets were brought into play; horses and cattle belonging to the settlers were spirited away; and several of the colonists were placed under arrest on trumped-up charges. These dastardly tactics were followed by an organized attempt to raid the settlement. On June 25 a troop of Bois Brûlés gathered on horseback, armed to the teeth and led by Alexander Macdonell and a half-breed named Cuthbert Grant. The settlers, though mustering barely one-half the strength of the raiders, resolved to make a stand, and placed themselves under the command of John M'Leod, a trader in the service of the Hudson's Bay Company. The Bois Brûlés bore down upon the settlement in menacing array. The colonists took what shelter they could find and prepared for battle. Fighting coolly, they made their shots tell. The advancing column hesitated and halted in dismay at the courage of the defenders. Then John M'Leod

remembered a cannon which was rusting un-
used at the small post which the Hudson's Bay
Company had on the river.   Hugh M'Lean
and two others were ordered to haul this to
the blacksmith's shanty.   The three men soon
found the cannon, and set it up in the smithy.
For shot, cart chains were chopped into
sections ; and the Bois Brûlés were treated to
a raking volley of ' chain shot.'   This was
something they had not looked for ; their
courage failed them, and they galloped out
of range.

But the remnant of Lord Selkirk's settlers
who had dared to linger on the Red River
were at the end of their resources.   Taking
counsel together, they resolved to quit the
colony.   They launched their boats on the
river, and followed the canoe route which led
to Hudson Bay.   They were accompanied by
a band of Indians of the Saulteaux tribe as far
as the entrance to Lake Winnipeg.   From
there a short journey placed them outside the
boundaries of Assiniboia.   When they arrived
at the northern end of Lake Winnipeg they
found a temporary refuge, in the vicinity of
Norway House, on the Jack river.

Alexander Macdonell and his Bois Brûlés
were now free utterly to blot out Colony

Gardens. They visited every part of the settlement and set fire to everything. Not a single house was left standing. Cabins, storehouses, the colony's grinding mill—all were reduced to a mass of ruins. Cameron's duplicity had been crowned with success; Alexander Macdonell's armed marauders had finished the task; Lord Selkirk's colony of farmers-in-the-making was scattered far and wide. Nevertheless, the Nor'westers were not undisputed masters of the situation. In the Hudson's Bay smithy, but ten feet square, four men continued the struggle. John M'Leod, James M'Intosh, and Archibald Currie, of the Hudson's Bay Company, defended their trading-post, with the assistance of 'noble Hugh M'Lean,' the only settler remaining on the Red River banks. By day and by night these men were forced to keep watch and ward. Whenever the Bois Brûlés drew near, the 'chain shot' drove them hurriedly to cover. At length the enemy withdrew, and M'Leod and his comrades walked out to survey the scene of desolation.

CHAPTER VIII

COLIN ROBERTSON, THE AVENGER

THREE years of self-sacrificing effort seemed to have been wasted. The colony of Assiniboia was no more ; its site was free to wandering redskins and greedy traders. Yet, at the very time when the colonists were being dispersed, succour was not far off. Lord Selkirk had received alarming news some time before, and at his solicitation Colin Robertson had hired a band of voyageurs, and was speeding forward with them to defend the settlement. Since 1811, when we saw him recruiting settlers for Lord Selkirk in Scotland, Colin Robertson had been in the service of the Hudson's Bay Company. Having been a servant of the Nor'westers he knew the value of Canadian canoemen in the fur trade, and, on his advice, the Hudson's Bay Company now imitated its rival by employing voyageurs. In temperament Colin was dour but audacious, a common type among the men of the Outer

Hebrides, and he had a grievance to avenge. He was sprung from the Robertson clan, which did not easily forget or forgive. He still remembered his quarrel with Crooked-armed Macdonald on the Saskatchewan. In his mind was the goading thought that he was a cast-off servant of the North-West Company; and he yearned for the day when he might exact retribution for his injuries, some of them real, some fancied.

It thus happened that before the final crisis came help was well on the way. When the party of rescuers arrived, the charred and deserted dwellings of Colony Gardens told their wordless story. They had come too late. It is quite possible that the newcomers had met by the way the throng of settlers who were bound for Canada, or at least had heard of their departure from the Red River. It is less likely that before arriving they had learned of the destruction of the settlement. A portion of the colonists still remained in the country, and Colin Robertson thought that he might yet save the situation. He had done all that Lord Selkirk had instructed him to do, and he now took further action on his own initiative. At his command the sun-tanned voyageurs descended to the river bank and launched their light canoes on the current. Down-stream, and northward along Lake Winnipeg, the party travelled, until they reached the exiles' place of refuge on the Jack river.

Robertson's resolute demeanour inspired the settlers with new courage, and they decided to go back with him and rebuild their homes. Before the summer was spent they were once more on the Red River. To their surprise the plots of ground which they had sown along the banks had suffered less than they had expected. During their absence John M'Leod had watchfully husbanded the precious crops, and from the land he so carefully tended fifteen hundred bushels of wheat were realized—the first ' bumper ' crop garnered within the borders of what are now the prairie provinces of Canada. M'Leod had built fences, had cut and stacked the matured hay, and had even engaged men to erect new buildings and to repair some of those which had escaped utter destruction. Near the spot where the colonists had landed in 1812 he had selected an appropriate site and had begun to erect a large domicile for the governor. ' It was of two stories,' wrote M'Leod in his diary, 'with main timbers of oak; a good substantial house.'

John M'Leod was a man of faith. He expected that Lord Selkirk's colony would soon be again firmly on its feet, and he was not to be disappointed. A fourth contingent of settlers arrived during the month of October 1815, having left Scotland in the spring. This band comprised upwards of ninety persons, nearly all natives of Kildonan. These were the most energetic body of settlers so far enlisted by the Earl of Selkirk. They experienced, of course, great disappointment on their arrival. Instead of finding a flourishing settlement, they saw the ruins of the habitations of their predecessors, and found that many friends whom they hoped would greet them had been enticed or driven away.

Along with these colonists came an important dignitary sent out by the Hudson's Bay Company. The 'Adventurers of England trading into Hudson's Bay' were now alarmed regarding the outlook for furs in the interior, and the general court of their stockholders had taken a new and important step. It was decided to appoint a resident governor-in-chief, with power not merely over the colony of Assiniboia, but over all the company's trading-posts as well. The man chosen to fill this office was Robert Semple, a British army captain on the retired list. He was a man of upright character and bull-dog courage, but he lacked the patience and diplomacy necessary for the problem with which he had to deal. Another to arrive with the contingent was Elder James Sutherland, who had been authorized by the Church of Scotland to baptize and to perform the marriage ceremony.

The occupants of Fort Gibraltar viewed the replanting of the settlement with baleful resentment. Their ranks were augmented during the autumn by a wayfarer from the east who hung up his musket at the fort and assumed control. This was none other than Duncan Cameron, returned from Canada, with the plaudits of some of his fellow-partners still ringing in his ears. To Colin Robertson the presence of Cameron at Fort Gibraltar was not of happy augury for the settlers' welfare. Robertson decided on prompt and radical action. In a word, he determined to take the Nor'westers' post by surprise. His raid was successful. The field-pieces and the property of the colonists which had been carried away in June were recovered.

Cameron himself was made a prisoner. But he was not held long. The man was a born actor and a smooth talker. In all seeming humility he now made specious promises of future good behaviour, and was allowed to return to his fort.

The houses of the colonists were ranged in succession along the Red River until they reached an elevated spot called Frog Plain. Some of the houses appear to have been situated on Frog Plain as well. Along the river, running north and south, was a road worn smooth by constant traffic. The spacious residence for the governor reared by John M'Leod, and the other buildings grouped about it, were surrounded by a strong palisade. To the whole the name of Fort Douglas was now given. In spite, however, of their seeming prosperity, the settlers found it necessary to migrate for the winter to the basin of the Pembina in order to obtain food. But again they found that the buffalo were many miles from Fort Daer, and the insufficiently clad winterers suffered greatly. They were disturbed, too, by frequent rumours of coming danger. The 'New Nation,' as the half-breeds chose to call themselves, were gathering, it was said, from every quarter, and with the breaking up of winter would descend like a scourge upon the colony.

The trouble brewing for the settlement was freely discussed among the Nor'westers. About the middle of March 1816 Alexander Macdonell sent a note to Duncan Cameron from Fort Qu'Appelle. ' A storm is gathering in the north,' declared Macdonell, ' ready to burst on the rascals who deserve it ; little do they know their situation. Last year was but a joke. The New Nation under their leaders are coming forward to clear their native soil of intruders and assassins.' A few words written at the same time by Cuthbert Grant show how the plans of the Bois Brûlés were maturing. ' The Half-breeds of Fort des Prairies and English River are all to be here in the spring,' he asserted ; ' it is to be hoped we shall come off with flying colours.'

Early in 1816 Governor Semple, who had been at Fort Daer, returned to Fort Douglas. Apparently he entertained no wholesome fears of the impending danger, for, instead of trying to conciliate his opponents, he embittered them by new acts of aggression. In April, for the second time, Colin Robertson, acting on the governor's instructions, captured Fort

Gibraltar. Again was Duncan Cameron taken prisoner, and this time he was held. It was decided that he should be carried to England for trial. In charge of Colin Robertson, Cameron was sent by canoe to York Factory. But no vessel of the Hudson's Bay Company was leaving for England during the summer of 1816, and the prisoner was detained until the following year. When at length he was brought to trial, it was found impossible to convict him of any crime, and he was discharged. Subsequently Cameron entered a suit against Lord Selkirk for illegal detention, asking damages, and the court awarded him £3000.

Shortly after Colin Robertson had departed with his prisoner, Governor Semple decided to dismantle Fort Gibraltar, and towards the end of May thirty men were sent to work to tear it down. Its encircling rampart was borne to the river and formed into a raft. Upon this the salvage of the demolished fort— a great mass of structural material—was driven down-stream to Fort Douglas and there utilized.

The tempest which Alexander Macdonell had presaged burst upon the colony soon after this demolition of Fort Gibraltar. The

incidents leading up to an outbreak of
hostilities have been narrated by Pierre
Pambrun, a French Canadian.   In April Pambrun had been commissioned by Governor
Semple to go to the Hudson's Bay fort on
the Qu'Appelle river.   Hard by this was
the Nor'westers' trading-post, called Fort
Qu'Appelle.   Pambrun remarks upon the
great number of half-breeds who had gathered
at the North-West Company's depot.   Many
of them had come from a great distance.
Some were from the upper Saskatchewan ;
others were from Cumberland House, situated
near the mouth of the same river.   Pambrun
says that during the first days of May he went
eastward along with George Sutherland, a
factor of the Hudson's Bay Company on the
Qu'Appelle, and a number of Sutherland's
men.   The party journeyed in five boats, and
had with them twenty-two bales of furs and
six hundred bags of pemmican.   On May 12
they were attacked on their way down the
river by an armed force of forty-nine Nor'-
westers, under the leadership of Cuthbert
Grant and Peter Pangman.   All were made
prisoners and conducted back to Fort
Qu'Appelle, where they were told by Alexander Macdonell that the seizure had been

made because of Colin Robertson's descent upon Fort Gibraltar. After five days' imprisonment George Sutherland and the servants of the Hudson's Bay Company were released. This did not mean, however, any approach of peace. Pierre Pambrun was still held in custody. Before the close of May Macdonell caused the furs and provisions which his men had purloined from Sutherland's party to be placed in boats, and he began to move down the Qu'Appelle, taking Pambrun with him. A band of Bois Brûlés on their horses kept pace with the boats. At the confluence of the Qu'Appelle and the Assiniboine Macdonell made a speech to a body of Saulteaux, and endeavoured to induce some of them to join his expedition to the Red River. The Hudson's Bay post of Brandon House, farther along the Assiniboine, was captured by Cuthbert Grant, with about twenty-five men under his command, and stripped of all its stores. Then the combined force of half-breeds, French Canadians, and Indians, in round numbers amounting to one hundred and twenty men, advanced to Portage la Prairie. They reached this point on or about June 16, and proceeded to make it a stronghold. They arranged bales of pemmican to form a rude fortification and planted two brass swivel-guns for defence. They were preparing for war, for the Nor'-westers had now resolved finally to uproot Lord Selkirk's colony from the banks of the Red River.

CHAPTER IX

SEVEN OAKS

IN the meantime, far removed from the Red River, other events bearing upon this story were happening. The Earl of Selkirk had had many troubles, and early in 1815 he was again filled with anxiety by news received in Scotland concerning the imperilled condition of Assiniboia. In consequence of these evil tidings he was led to petition Lord Bathurst, secretary for War and the Colonies in the administration of Lord Liverpool, and to ask that some protection should be afforded his colonists, who were loyal subjects of the crown. Lord Bathurst acted promptly. He wrote in March to Sir Gordon Drummond, administrator of the government of Canada, saying that Lord Selkirk's request should be granted and that action should be taken in Canada to protect the colony. But Sir Gordon Drummond, after looking into the matter, decided not to grant the protection which

Selkirk desired. He had reasons, which he sent to the British minister.

By this time the affairs of his colony had come to such a sorry pass that Lord Selkirk felt it necessary to travel to America. Accordingly, in the autumn of 1815, he embarked for New York, accompanied by Lady Selkirk and his three children, Dunbar, Isabella, and Katherine. Arriving on November 15, he heard for the first time of the overthrow of his colony through the machinations of Duncan Cameron and Alexander Macdonell. At once he hastened to Montreal, where he received from eye-witnesses a more detailed version of the occurrence. Many of the settlers brought to the east were indignant at the treatment they had received at the hands of the Nor'westers and were prepared to testify against them. In view of this, Lord Selkirk applied to magistrates at York (Toronto) and Montreal, desiring that affidavits should be taken from certain of the settlers with respect to their experiences on the Red River. In this way he hoped to accumulate a mass of evidence which should strengthen his plea for military assistance from the Canadian government. Among those whom Selkirk met in Montreal was

Miles Macdonell. The former governor of Assiniboia was then awaiting trial on charges brought against him by officers of the North-West Company. He was never tried, however, for the charges were dropped later on.

In November Lord Selkirk saw Sir Gordon Drummond and urged that help be sent to Assiniboia. From this time until the expiration of Drummond's term of office (May 1816) a correspondence on this question was kept up between the two men. No steps, however, were taken by Drummond to accede to Selkirk's wishes, nor did he inform Selkirk officially why his requests were denied. During the winter news of the restoration of the colony was brought to Selkirk by a French Canadian named Laguimonière, who had travelled two thousand miles on foot with the information. On receipt of this news Selkirk became even more urgent in his appeals for armed assistance. ' If, however, your Excellency,' he wrote to Drummond on April 23, ' persevere in your intention to do nothing till you receive further instructions, there is a probability almost amounting to a certainty that another season must be lost before the requisite force can be sent up—during another year the settlers must remain exposed to

attack, and there is every reason to expect that
in consequence of this delay many lives may
be lost.'

Lord Selkirk wished to send a message of
encouragement to his people in the colony.
Laguimonière, the wonderful Canadian wood-
runner, would carry it. He wrote a number
of letters, telling of his arrival in Canada,
giving assurance of his deep concern for the
settlement's welfare, and promising to come
to the aid of the colonists as soon as the rivers
were free of ice, with whatever force he could
muster. Bearing these letters, the messenger
set out on his journey over the wild spaces
between Montreal and the Red River. In
some way his mission became known to the
Nor'westers at Fort William, for on June 3
Archibald Norman M'Leod, a partner of the
North-West Company, issued an order that
Selkirk's courier should be intercepted. Near
Fond du Lac, at the western end of Lake
Superior, Laguimonière was waylaid and
robbed. The letters which he carried were
taken to Fort William, where several of them
were found later.

As we have seen in the last chapter, it was
in this same month that Alexander Macdonell,
at Portage la Prairie, was organizing his half-

breeds for a raid on Fort Douglas. His brigade, as finally made up, consisted of about seventy Bois Brûlés, Canadians, and Indians, all well armed and mounted. As soon as these troopers were ready to advance, Macdonell surrendered the leadership to Cuthbert Grant, deeming it wise not to take part in the raid himself. The marauders then marched out in the direction of the settlement.

The settlers in the meantime were not wholly oblivious of the danger threatening them. There was a general feeling of insecurity in the colony, and a regular watch had been instituted at Fort Douglas to guard against a surprise attack. Governor Semple, however, did not seem to take a very serious view of the situation. He was about to depart to York Factory on business. But a rough awakening came. On June 17 two Cree Indians arrived at Fort Douglas with the alarming tidings that in two days an attack would be made upon the settlement.[1]

About five o'clock in the afternoon of June 19, a boy who was stationed in the watch-

[1] For the details of the tragedy which now occurred we are chiefly indebted to the accounts of John Pritchard, a former Nor'wester, who had settled with his family at the Red River, of Michael Heden, a blacksmith connected with the settlement, and of John Bourke, the colony store-keeper.

house of the fort cried out that he saw a party of half-breeds approaching. Thereupon Governor Semple hurried to the watch-house and scanned the plains through a glass. He saw a troop of horsemen moving towards the Red River—evidently heading for a point some distance to the north of Fort Douglas.

'We must go out to meet these people,' said Governor Semple: 'let twenty men follow me.'

There was a prompt response to the call, and Semple led his volunteers out of the fort and towards the advancing horsemen. He had not gone far when he met a number of colonists, running towards Fort Douglas and shouting in wild excitement:

'The half-breeds! the half-breeds!'

Governor Semple now sent John Bourke back to Fort Douglas for one of the guns, and instructed him to bring up whatever men could be spared from among those garrisoning the fort. The advance party halted to wait until these should arrive; but at length Semple grew impatient and ordered his men to advance without them. The Nor'westers had concealed themselves behind a clump of trees. As Semple approached they galloped out, extended their line into a half-moon formation, and bore down to meet him. They were dressed as Indian warriors and painted in hideous fashion. The force was well equipped with guns, knives, bows and arrows, and spears.

A solitary horseman emerged from the hostile squadron and rode towards Governor Semple. This was François Boucher, a French-Canadian clerk in the employ of the North-West Company, son of a tavern-keeper in Montreal. Ostensibly his object was to parley with the governor. Boucher waved his hand, shouting aloud :

' What do you want ? '

Semple took his reply from the French Canadian's mouth. ' What do *you* want ? ' he questioned in plainer English.

' We want our fort,' said Boucher.

' Go to your fort,' answered Semple.

' Why did you destroy our fort, you d—d rascal ? ' exclaimed the French Canadian.

The two were now at close quarters, and Governor Semple had seized the bridle of Boucher's horse.

' Scoundrel, do you tell me so ? ' he said.

Pritchard says that the governor grasped Boucher's gun, no doubt expecting an attack upon his person. The French Canadian leapt from his horse, and at this instant a shot rang out from the column of the Nor'westers. Lieutenant Holt, a clerk in the colony's service, fell struggling upon the ground. Boucher ran in the direction of his own party, and soon there was the sound of another musket. This time Governor Semple was struck in the thigh. He called at once to his men :

' Do what you can to take care of yourselves.'

The band ignored this behest, and gathered round him to ascertain the extent of his injury. The Nor'westers now began to bring the two ends of their column together, and soon Semple's party was surrounded. The fact that their foe was now helpless did not keep the Nor'westers from pouring in a destructive fire. Most of Semple's men fell at the first volley. The few left standing pulled off their hats and begged for mercy. A certain Captain Rogers hastened towards the line of the Nor'westers and threw up his hands. He was followed by John Pritchard. One of the Bois Brûlés shot Rogers in the head and another rushed on him and stabbed him with a knife. Luckily Pritchard was confronted by a French Canadian, named

Augustin Lavigne, whom he had formerly known and who now protected him from butchery.

The wounded governor lay stretched upon the ground. Supporting his head with his hand, he addressed Cuthbert Grant :

' I am not mortally wounded,' he said, ' and if you could get me conveyed to the fort, I think I should live.'

Grant promised to comply with the request. He left the governor in charge of one of his men and went away, but during his absence an Indian approached and shot Semple to death.

Meanwhile John Bourke had gone back for a field-piece and for reinforcements. Bourke reached the fort, but after he had placed the small cannon in a cart he was permitted by those in the fort to take only one man away with him. He and his companion began to drag the cart down the road. Suddenly they were startled by the sound of the musketry fire in the distance which had struck down Semple's party. Fearing lest they might lose the gun, the pair turned back towards the fort. On their way they were met by ten men from Fort Douglas, hurrying to the scene of the conflict. Bourke told his comrade to take the field-piece inside the fort, and himself joined the rescue party. But they were too late: when they arrived at the scene of the struggle they could effect nothing.

'Give up your arms,' was the command of the Nor'westers.

The eleven men, seeing that resistance on their part would be useless, took to their heels. The Nor'westers fired ; one of the fleeing men was killed and John Bourke was severely wounded. For the numbers engaged the carnage was terrible. Of the party which had left Fort Douglas with Governor Semple there were but six survivors. Michael Heden and Daniel M'Kay had run to the riverside during the *mêlée*. They succeeded in getting across in a canoe and arrived at Fort Douglas the same night. Michael Kilkenny and George Sutherland escaped by swimming the river. In addition to John Pritchard, another prisoner, Anthony Macdonell, had been spared. The total number of the dead was twenty-three. Among the slain were Rogers, the governor's secretary, Doctor Wilkinson, Alexander M'Lean, the most enterprising settler in the colony, and Surgeon James White. The Irish colonists suffered severely in proportion to their number: they lost seven in all. The Nor'westers had one man killed and one wounded. This sanguinary encounter, which took place beside the highway leading along the Red River to Frog Plain, is known as the massacre of Seven Oaks.

There was much disappointment among the Nor'westers when they learned that Colin Robertson was not in the colony. Cuthbert Grant vowed that Robertson would have been scalped had he been captured. 'They would have cut his body into small bits,' said Pritchard, 'and boiled it afterwards for the dogs.' Pritchard himself was carried as a prisoner to Frog Plain, where the Nor'westers made their encampment. A savage spirit had been aroused. Pritchard found that even yet the lust for blood had not been sated, and that it would be necessary to plead for the wives and children of the colonists. He remonstrated with Cuthbert Grant and urged him not to forget that the women of the settlement were of his dead father's people. At length the half-breed leader softened, and agreed that Pritchard should act as a mediator. Grant was willing that the settlers should go in peace, if the public property of the colony were given up. Pritchard made three trips between Grant's headquarters and the fort before an agreement was reached. 'On my arrival at the fort,' he said, 'what a scene of distress presented itself! The widows, children and relations of the slain, in horrors of despair, were lamenting the dead,[1] and were trembling for the safety of the survivors.'

On the morning of June 20 Cuthbert Grant himself, with over a score of his followers, went to Fort Douglas. It was then agreed that the settlers should abandon their homes and that the fort should be evacuated. An inventory was made of the goods of the colony, and the terms of surrender were signed by Cuthbert Grant as a clerk and representative of the North-West Company. Contrary to Grant's promises, the private effects of the colonists were overhauled and looted. Michael Heden records that even his clothes and blankets were stolen.

On the evening of the same day a messenger presented himself at Portage la Prairie bringing Alexander Macdonell an account of the massacre. Pierre Pambrun declares that

---

[1] Some of the dead were afterwards taken from the field of Seven Oaks to Fort Douglas by Cree and Saulteaux Indians. These received decent burial, but the others, lying uninterred as they had fallen, became a prey to the wild beasts of the prairie.

Macdonell and others who were with him became hilarious with joy. 'Good news,' shouted Macdonell in French, as he conveyed the tidings to his associates.

Again disaster had overtaken Lord Selkirk's plans. The second desolation of his colony and expulsion of his colonists occurred on June 22, 1816. The evicted people set out in canoes down the Red River. Michael Heden and John Bourke both declared that the number of those who embarked was approximately two hundred. This total would appear, however, to be much too large, unless additions had been made to the colony of which we have no documentary evidence. Some French-Canadian families had settled at ' the Forks,' it is true, but these were not numerous enough to bring the population of the settlement to two hundred persons, leaving uncounted the number who had lately perished.

On June 24, as the exiles were proceeding down the river, they met nine or ten canoes and one bateau. In these were almost a hundred armed Nor'westers under the command of Archibald Norman M'Leod of Fort William. M'Leod's purpose was apparently to assist in the extermination of the colony. His first question of the party travelling northward was ' whether that rascal and scoundrel Robertson was in the boats.' When he was told of the calamity which had befallen Governor Semple and his band, he ordered all the exiles ashore. By virtue of his office as a magistrate for the Indian Territories he wished to examine them.[1]

He searched the baggage belonging to the evicted settlers and scrutinized their books and papers. ' Those who play at bowls,' remarked ' Justice ' M'Leod, ' must expect to meet with rubbers.' Pritchard was told to write his version of the recent transactions at ' the Forks,' and did so ; but his account did not please M'Leod. ' You have drawn up a pretty paper,' he grumbled ; ' you had better take care of yourself, or you will get into a scrape.'

Michael Heden also was examined as to his knowledge of the matter. When M'Leod heard the answers of Heden he was even more wrathful.

' They are all lies,' he declared with emphasis.

---

[1] An act of the Imperial parliament of 1803 had transferred jurisdiction in the case of offences committed in the Indian Territories from Great Britain to Canada, and had allowed the Canadian authorities to appoint magistrates for these rather undefined regions. M'Leod was one of these magistrates.

The result of M'Leod's judicial procedure was that five of the party were detained and placed under arrest. The others were allowed to proceed on their way. John Bourke was charged with felony, and Michael Heden and Patrick Corcoran were served with subpœnas to give evidence for the crown against him, on September 1, at Montreal. John Pritchard and Daniel M'Kay were among the five detained, presumably as crown witnesses. After some delay—M'Leod had to visit Fort Douglas and the neighbourhood—the prisoners were sent on the long journey to Fort William on Lake Superior. Bourke was at once stripped of his valuables and placed in irons, regardless of the fact that his wound was causing him intense suffering. During the whole of the journey he was compelled to lie manacled on a pile of baggage in one of the canoes.

Fort Douglas on the Red River was still standing, but the character of its occupants had changed radically. At first Cuthbert Grant took command, but he soon made way for Alexander Macdonell, who reached Fort Douglas shortly after the affair at Seven Oaks. When Archibald Norman M'Leod appeared, he was the senior officer in authority, and he took up his residence in the apartments of the late Governor Semple. One day M'Leod and some followers rode over to an encampment of Crees and Saulteaux near the ruins of Fort Gibraltar. Here M'Leod collected and harangued the Indians. He upbraided them for their failure to interfere when Duncan Cameron had been forcibly removed to Hudson Bay, and he spoke harshly of their sympathy for the colonists when the Nor'-westers had found it necessary to drive them away. Peguis, chief of the Saulteaux and the leading figure in the Indian camp, listened attentively, but remained stolidly taciturn. On the evening of the same day the Nor'-westers returned to Fort Douglas and indulged in some of their wildest revelries. The Bois Brûlés stripped themselves naked and celebrated their recent triumph in a wild and savage orgy, while their more staid companions looked on with approval.

According to the testimony of Augustin Lavigne, M'Leod during his stay at Fort Douglas publicly made the following promise to an assembly of Bois Brûlés : ' My kinsmen, my comrades, who have helped us in the time of need ; I have brought clothing for you   I expected to have found about forty of you here with Mr Macdonell, but there are more of you. I have forty suits of clothing. Those who are most in need of them may have these, and on the arrival of the canoes in autumn, the rest of you shall be clothed likewise.'

CHAPTER X

WE left Lord Selkirk at Montreal. Several days before the massacre of Seven Oaks he had completed the preparations for his journey to the west, and was hastening forward in the hope of arriving at the Red River in time to save his colony. He had secured his own appointment as justice of the peace for Upper Canada and the Indian Territories, and also the promise of a bodyguard of one non-commissioned officer and six men for his personal defence. This much he had obtained from the Canadian authorities. They remained unwilling, however, to send armed aid to Assiniboia. This want Lord Selkirk was himself supplying, for he was bringing with him a fresh contingent of settlers—of a class hitherto unknown among his colonists. These new settlers were trained soldiers, disciplined and tried in active service on many a battle-field.

The close of the War of 1812 by the Treaty of Ghent, signed on December 24, 1814, had left in Canada several battalions of regular soldiers under colours. In the early summer of 1816 orders were issued that the De Meuron regiment, in barracks at Montreal, and the Watteville regiment, stationed at Kingston, should be honourably disbanded. These regiments were composed of Swiss, Italian, and other mercenaries who had fought for Great Britain in her struggle with Napoleon. In 1809 the De Meuron regiment had been sent from Gibraltar to the island of Malta. In 1813 it had been transported to Canada with the reputation of being ' as fine and well-appointed a regiment as any in his Majesty's service.' It consisted of more than a thousand men, with seventy-five officers. The Watteville regiment, a force equally large, had landed at Quebec on June 10, 1813. Its ensign indicated that it had been in the campaigns waged against France in the Spanish peninsula and had served under Sir John Stuart in southern Italy.

About two hundred of the disbanded De Meurons desired to remain in Canada, and Selkirk at once sought to interest them in his western enterprise. Four officers—Captains

Matthey and D'Orsonnens and Lieutenants Graffenreid and Fauché—and about eighty of the rank and file were willing to enlist. It was agreed that they should receive allotments of land in Assiniboia on the terms granted to the settlers who had formerly gone from Scotland and Ireland. They were to be supplied with the necessary agricultural implements, and each was to be given a musket for hunting or for defence. Their wages were to be eight dollars a month for manning the boats which should take them to their destination. In case the settlement should not be to their liking, Lord Selkirk pledged himself to transport them to Europe free of cost, by way of either Montreal or Hudson Bay.

On June 4 the contingent of men and officers began their journey from Montreal up the St Lawrence. At Kingston a halt was made while Captain Matthey, acting for the Earl of Selkirk, enlisted twenty more veterans of the Watteville regiment. It is stated that an officer and several privates from another disbanded regiment, the Glengarry Fencibles, were also engaged as settlers, but it is not clear at what point they joined the party. When all was ready for the long journey, the combined forces skirted the northern shore of Lake Ontario from Kingston, until they reached York, the capital of Upper Canada. Thence their route lay to Georgian Bay by way of Lake Simcoe and the Severn.

Lord Selkirk left Montreal on June 16, following in the wake of his new-won colonists, and overtook them at the entrance into Georgian Bay. Apparently he went over the same route, for he crossed Lake Simcoe. Information is lacking as to his companions. Miles Macdonell could not have been with him, for Macdonell had been sent forward earlier with a small body of men in light canoes that he might reach the settlement in advance of Lord Selkirk. One hundred and twenty Canadian voyageurs had been recently engaged to go to Assiniboia in the service of the Hudson's Bay Company. Possibly these canoemen accompanied Selkirk on the first stages of his journey.

On Drummond Island, at the head of Lake Huron, was situated the most westerly military station maintained by the government of Upper Canada. Here Lord Selkirk halted and allowed his company to go on in advance into the straits of St Mary. At the military post at Drummond Island he was furnished with the promised escort of six men under a non-commissioned officer of the 37th regiment. On July 22 he was present at a council held on the island by the Indian authorities stationed there. One of the principal figures at this council was Katawabetay, chief of the Chippewas, from Sand Lake. On being questioned, Katawabetay told of his refusal the year before to join the Nor'westers in an attack on the Red River Colony; he also declared that an attempt had been made during the previous spring by a trader named Grant to have some of his young Chippewas waylay Lord Selkirk's messenger, Laguimonière, near Fond du Lac. Grant had offered Katawabetay two kegs of rum and some tobacco, but the bribe was refused. The Ottawa Indians, not the Chippewas, had waylaid the messenger. This trader Grant had told Katawabetay that he was going to the Red River ' to fight the settlers.' [1]

Lord Selkirk put a question to Katawabetay.

' Are the Indians about the Red River, or that part of the country you come from,' asked the earl through an interpreter, ' pleased

[1] The trader was probably Charles Grant, a clerk in the North-West Company's fort at Fond du Lac, and not Cuthbert Grant, the leader at Seven Oaks.

or displeased at the people settling at the Red
River ? '

'At the commencement of the settlement
at Red River, some of the Indians did not
like it,' answered the chief, ' but at present
they are all glad of its being settled.'

Meanwhile the party which had gone on in
advance had entered the St Mary's river,
connecting Lakes Huron and Superior, had
crossed the half-mile portage of the Sault
Rapids, and had pitched their camp some
distance farther up-stream. Before the end
of July Lord Selkirk was again among them.
He gave the order to advance, and the boats
were launched. But, only a few miles out from
Sault Ste Marie, there suddenly appeared two
canoes, in one of which was Miles Macdonell.
For the first time Lord Selkirk now learned of
the disaster which had befallen the colony in
the month of June. Macdonell had gone as far
as the mouth of the Winnipeg before he learned
the news. Now he was able to tell Lord Selkirk
of the massacre of Semple and his men, of the
eviction of the settlers, and of the forcible
detention of those sent by M'Leod to the
Nor'westers' trading-post at Fort William.

Selkirk had entertained the hope of avert-
ing a calamity at the settlement by bringing

in enough retired soldiers to preserve order. But this hope was now utterly blasted. He might, however, use the resources of the law against the traders at Fort William, and this he decided to attempt. He was, however, in a peculiar position. He had, it is true, been created a justice of the peace, but it would seem hardly proper for him to try law-breakers who were attacking his own personal interests. Accordingly, before finally setting out for Fort William, he begged Magistrate John Askin, of Drummond Island, and Magistrate Ermatinger, of Sault Ste Marie, to accompany him. But neither of these men could leave his duties. When Selkirk thus failed to secure disinterested judges, he determined to act under the authority with which he had been vested. In a letter, dated July 29, to Sir John Sherbrooke, the recently appointed governor of Canada, he referred with some uneasiness to the position in which he found himself. ' I am therefore reduced to the alternative of acting alone,' he wrote, ' or of allowing an audacious crime to pass unpunished. In these circumstances, I cannot doubt that it is my duty to act, though I am not without apprehension that the law may be openly resisted by a set of men who have been accustomed to consider force as the only criterion of right.'

Selkirk advanced to Fort William. There is no record of his journey across the deep sounds and along the rock-girt shores of Lake Superior. His contingent was divided into two sections, possibly as soon as it emerged from the St Mary's river and entered Whitefish Bay. Selkirk himself sped forward with the less cumbersome craft, while the soldier-settlers advanced more leisurely in their bateaux. Early in August the vanguard came within sight of the islands that bar the approach to Thunder Bay. Then, as their canoes slipped through the dark waters, they were soon abeam of that majestic headland, Thunder Cape, ' the agèd Cape of Storms.' Inside the bay they saw that long, low island known as the Sleeping Giant. A portion of the voyageurs, led by a Canadian named Chatelain, disembarked upon an island about seven miles from Fort William. Selkirk, with the rest of the advance party, went on. Skirting the settlement at Fort William, they ascended the river Kaministikwia for about half a mile, and on the opposite bank from the fort, at a spot since known as Point De Meuron, they erected their temporary habitations.

CHAPTER XI

FORT WILLIAM

FORT WILLIAM was the Mecca of the traders and voyageurs who served the North-West Company. It was the divisional point and the warehousing centre of sixty trading-posts. No less than five thousand persons were engaged in the trade which centred at Fort William. During the season from May to September the traffic carried on at the fort was of the most active character. A flotilla of boats and canoes would arrive from Lachine with multifarious articles of commerce for inland barter. These boats would then set out on their homeward journey laden with peltry gathered from far and near. Every season two or three of the principal partners of the company arrived at the fort from Montreal. They were ' hyperborean nabobs,' who travelled with whatever luxury wealth could afford them on the express service by lake and stream.

FORT WILLIAM

From an old print in the John Ross Robertson Collection, Toronto Public Library

At this time Fort William had the proportions of a good-sized village. Its structures were of wood and were of all shapes and sizes. One commodious building near the centre of the fort, fronted by a wide verandah, immediately caught the eye of the visitor. It contained a council - hall, the mercantile parliament-chamber of the Nor'westers. Under the same roof was a great banqueting-hall, in which two hundred persons could be seated. In this hall were wont to gather the notables of the North-West Company, and any guests who were fortunate enough to gain admission. Here, in the heart of the wilderness, there was no stint of food when the long tables were spread. Chefs brought from Montreal prepared savoury viands ; the brimming bowl was emptied and too often replenished ; and the songs of this deep-throated race of merchantmen pealed to the rafters until revelry almost ended in riot. At one end of the room stood the bust of Simon M'Tavish, placed so that his gaze seemed to rest upon the proprietors and servants of the company he had called into being. About the walls hung numerous portraits—one of the reigning monarch, George III, another of the Prince Regent, a third of Admiral Lord

Nelson. Here, too, was a painting of the famous battle of the Nile, and a wonderful map of the fur-bearing country, the work of the intrepid explorer David Thompson.

The unexpected appearance of Lord Selkirk in the vicinity of Fort William found the Nor'westers off their guard and created a great sensation. It was a matter of common knowledge among the Nor'westers that Selkirk was on his way to the Red River with a squad of armed men, but they understood that he would follow the route leading past their fort at Fond du Lac. There is evidence to show that a plot to compass Selkirk's death or seizure had been mooted some weeks before. John Bourke, on the road to Fort William as a prisoner, had overheard a conversation between Alexander Macdonell and several other partners of the North-West Company. This conversation had occurred at night, not far from Rainy Lake. According to the story, Bourke was lying on the ground, seemingly asleep, when the partners, standing by a camp-fire, fell to discussing their recent coup at 'the Forks.' Their talk drifted to the subject of Lord Selkirk's proposed visit to Assiniboia, and Macdonell assured the others

SIMON M'TAVISH, FOUNDER OF THE
NORTH-WEST COMPANY

From a water-colour drawing in M'Gill University Library

that the North-West Company had nothing to fear from Selkirk, and that if extreme measures were necessary Selkirk should be quietly assassinated. 'The half-breeds,' he declared, 'will take him while he is asleep, early in the morning.' Macdonell went so far as to mention the name of a Bois Brûlé who would be willing to bring Lord Selkirk down with his musket, if necessary.

Bourke told to his fellow-prisoners, Patrick Corcoran and Michael Heden, what he had overheard. It thus happened that when Heden now learned that the founder of Assiniboia was actually camping on the Kaministikwia, he became alarmed for his safety. Though a prisoner, he seems to have had some liberty of movement. At any rate, he was able to slip off alone and to launch a small boat. Once afloat, he rowed to the island where Chatelain and his voyageurs had halted on the way to Fort William. The water was boisterous, and Heden had great difficulty in piloting his craft. He gained the island, however, and told Chatelain of his fear that Lord Selkirk might come to harm. Heden returned to the fort, and was there taken to task and roughly handled for his temerity in going to see one of Lord Selkirk's servants.

On August 12 the second section of the contingent arrived with the experienced campaigners. From. the moment they raised their tents Lord Selkirk began to show a bold front against the Nor'westers. Captain D'Orsonnens was entrusted on the day of his arrival with a letter from Selkirk to William M'Gillivray, the most prominent partner at Fort William. In this M'Gillivray was asked his reason for holding in custody various persons whose names were given, and was requested to grant their immediate release. M'Gillivray was surprisingly conciliatory. He permitted several of the persons named in the letter to proceed at once to Selkirk's camp, and assured Lord Selkirk that they had never been prisoners. John Bourke and Michael Heden he still retained, because their presence was demanded in the courts at Montreal.

Acting as a justice of the peace, Selkirk now held a court in which he heard evidence from those whom M'Gillivray had surrendered. Before the day was over he had secured sufficient information, as he thought, to justify legal action against certain of the partners at Fort William. He decided to arrest William M'Gillivray first, and sent two men as constables with a warrant against

M'Gillivray. On the afternoon of August 13 these officers went down the river to the fort. Along with them went a guard of nine men fully armed. While the guard remained posted without, the constables entered the fort. They found M'Gillivray in his room writing a letter. He read the warrant which they thrust into his hand, and then without comment said that he was prepared to go with them. His only desire was that two partners, Kenneth M'Kenzie and Dr John M'Loughlin, might accompany him to furnish bail. The constables acceded to this request, and the three Nor'westers got into a canoe and were paddled to Point De Meuron.

The officers conducted their prisoners to the Earl of Selkirk's tent. When Selkirk learned that the two other partners of the North-West Company were also in his power, he resolved upon an imprudent act, one which can scarcely be defended. Not only did he refuse his prisoner bail ; he framed indictments against M'Kenzie and M'Loughlin and ordered the constables to take them in charge. A short examination of William M'Gillivray convinced Lord Selkirk that he would not be going beyond his powers were he to apprehend the remaining partners who were at Fort William. To accomplish this he drew up the necessary papers, and then sent the same constables to make the arrests. Twenty-five De Meuron soldiers under Captain D'Orsonnens and Lieutenant Fauché were detailed as an escort.

When the constables strode up the river bank to the fort to perform their official duty, they found a great throng of Canadians, half-breeds, and Indians gathered about the entrance. D'Orsonnens and the bulk of the escort remained behind on the river within easy call. Near the gateway the officers saw two of the partners whom they were instructed to apprehend, and immediately served them with warrants. A third partner, John M'Donald, made a sturdy show of resistance. He declaimed against the validity of the warrant, and protested that no stranger dare enter the fort until William M'Gillivray was set free. A scramble followed. Some of the Nor'-westers tried to close the gate, while the constables struggled to make their way inside. When one of the constables shouted lustily for aid, the bugle blew at the boats. This was by prearrangement the signal to Captain Matthey at Point De Meuron that the constables had met with opposition. The signal,

WILLIAM M'GILLIVRAY, A PARTNER IN THE
NORTH-WEST COMPANY

From a photograph in M'Gill University Library

however, proved unnecessary. In spite of the angry crowd at the entrance, Selkirk's men pushed open the gate of the fort. They seized M'Donald, who struggled fiercely, and bore him away towards the boats. The soldiers marched up from the boats, and, in a moment, Fort William was in their possession. Before further help arrived, in response to the bugle-call, the struggle was over. Six partners of the North-West Company were taken to the boats and carried to Lord Selkirk's encampment. These were John M'Donald, Daniel M'Kenzie, Allan M'Donald, Hugh M'Gillis, Alexander M'Kenzie, and Simon Fraser, the last named being the noted explorer. Captain D'Orsonnens stationed a guard within the fort, and himself remained behind to search the papers of those who had been arrested.

By the time Lord Selkirk had finished the examination of his fresh group of prisoners the hour was late. He did not wish to keep any of the partners in confinement, and so he arranged that they should go back to their quarters at the fort for the night. The prisoners promised that they would behave in seemly fashion, and do nothing of a hostile nature. There is evidence to show that before morning many papers were burned in the mess-room kitchen at the fort. Word was also brought to Lord Selkirk that a quantity of firearms and ammunition had been removed from Fort William during the night. In consequence of this information he issued another warrant, authorizing a ' search for arms.' When the search was made fifty or more guns and fowling-pieces were found hidden among some hay in a barn. Eight barrels of gunpowder were also found lying in a swampy place not far from the fort, and the manner in which the grass was trampled down indicated that the barrels had been deposited there very recently. When Selkirk learned of this attempt to remove arms and ammunition, he felt justified in adopting stringent measures. He ordered what was practically an occupation of Fort William. Most of the Canadians, Bois Brûlés, and Indians in the service of the North-West Company were commanded to leave the fort and to cross to the other side of the river. Their canoes were confiscated. The nine partners were held as prisoners and closely watched. Selkirk's force abandoned Point De Meuron and erected their tents on ground near Fort William. The hearing was continued, and it

was finally decided that the accused should
be committed for trial at York and conducted
thither under a strong guard.

Selkirk had not exceeded his authority as
a justice of the peace in holding the investiga-
tions and in sending the partners for trial to
the judicial headquarters of the province.
But he had also seized the property of the
North-West Company and driven its servants
from their fort, and this was straining his legal
powers. The task of taking the nine partners
to York was entrusted to Lieutenant Fauché.
Three canoes were provisioned for the journey.
Indians regularly employed by the North-
West Company were engaged as canoemen
and guides. On August 18 the party set out
from Fort William. At first the journey
went tranquilly enough. On the eighth day,
about one o'clock in the afternoon, the party
drew up their canoes on Isle au Parisien, in
Whitefish Bay, to take dinner. A heavy
westerly breeze sprang up, but they were on
the leeward side of the island and did not
notice its full strength. Lieutenant Fauché
had misgivings, however, and before he would
resume the journey he consulted his prisoner,
William M'Gillivray, who was an expert
canoeman. M'Gillivray was confident that

the 'traverse' to Sault Ste Marie could be made in safety if the Indian guides exercised great caution. The guides, on the other hand, objected to leaving the island. Their advice was not heeded, and the three canoes put out. Very soon they were running before a squall and shipping water. The first canoe turned its prow in the direction of Isle aux Erables, lying to the left, and the other two followed this example. Near Isle aux Erables there were some shoals destined now to cause tragic disaster. In attempting to pass these shoals the leading canoe was capsized. The others, so heavily laden that they could do nothing to rescue their companions, paddled hurriedly to shore, unloaded part of their cargoes, and then hastened to the spot where their comrades were struggling in the stormy waters. But it was too late. In spite of the most heroic efforts nine of the twenty-one persons belonging to the wrecked canoe were drowned. Kenneth M'Kenzie, of the North-West Company, was one of those who perished; six of the others were Indians; the remaining two were discharged soldiers. Another canoe was procured at Sault Ste Marie. The party continued its journey and reached York on September 3. Fauché at once sought the attorney-general, in order to take proper legal steps, but found that he was absent. The prisoners meanwhile applied for a writ of habeas corpus, and Fauché was instructed to take them to Montreal. This was to take them to the home of the Nor'westers, where they would be supported by powerful influences. On September 10, when the partners arrived in Montreal, they were at once admitted to bail.

Meanwhile, Lord Selkirk continued to exercise full sway over Fort William and its environs. He had himself no misgivings whatever with regard to the legality of his treatment of the Nor'westers. In his view he had taken possession of a place which had served, to quote his own words, ' the last of any in the British dominions, as an asylum for banditti and murderers, and the receptacle for their plunder.' During the ensuing winter he sent out expeditions to capture the posts belonging to the North-West Company at Michipicoten, Rainy Lake, and Fond du Lac. In March he commissioned a part of his followers to advance into the territory of Assiniboia to restore order. The veterans whom he sent artfully arranged their journey so that they should approach ' the Forks ' from the south.   The Nor'westers in Fort Douglas were wholly unaware that a foe was advancing against them.   On a blustering night, amid storm and darkness, Selkirk's men crept up to the walls, carrying ladders.   In a trice they had scaled the ramparts, and the fort was in their possession.

On the first day of May 1817 Lord Selkirk himself went forward to the west from Fort William, taking with him the bodyguard which he had procured at Drummond Island. He followed the fur traders' route up the Kaministikwia to Dog Lake, thence, by way of the waters which connect with Rainy Lake, on to the Lake of the Woods, and down the rushing Winnipeg.   After a journey of seven weeks he emerged from the forest-clad wilderness and saw for the first time the little row of farms which the toil of his long-suffering colonists had brought into being on the open plains.

CHAPTER XII

' THE parish shall be Kildonan.'

As Lord Selkirk spoke, he was standing in what is to-day the northern part of the city of Winnipeg. A large gathering of settlers listened to his words. The refugees of the year before, who were encamped on the Jack river, had returned to their homes, and now, in instituting a parish for them and creating the first local division in Assiniboia, Lord Selkirk was giving it a name reminiscent of the vales of Sutherlandshire. ' Here you shall build your church,' continued his lordship. The Earl of Selkirk's religion was deep-seated, and he was resolved to make adequate provision for public worship. ' And that lot,' he said, indicating a piece of ground across a rivulet known as Parsonage Creek, ' is for a school.' For his time he held what was advanced radical doctrine in regard to education, for he believed that there should be a common school in every parish.

Selkirk's genial presence and his magnanimity of character quickly banished any prejudices which the colonists had formed against him. In view of the hardships they had endured, he divided among them, free of all dues, some additional land. To the discharged soldiers he gave land on both sides of the river. They were to live not far removed from Fort Douglas, in order that they might give speedy aid in case of trouble. The settlers were enjoined to open roads, construct bridges, and build flour-mills at convenient places.

Meanwhile, the disturbances in the fur country were being considered in the motherland. When news of the Seven Oaks affair and of other acts of violence reached Great Britain, Lord Bathurst thought that the home government should take action. He sent an official note to Sir John Sherbrooke, the governor of Canada, instructing him to deal with the situation. Sherbrooke was to see that the forts, buildings, and property involved in the unhappy conflict should be restored to their rightful owners, and that illegal restrictions on trade should be removed. When Sherbrooke received this dispatch, in February 1817, he selected two military officers, Lieutenant - Colonel Coltman and Major Fletcher, to go to the Indian Territories in order to arbitrate upon the questions causing dissension. The two commissioners left Montreal in May, escorted by forty men of the 37th regiment. From Sault Ste Marie, Coltman journeyed on ahead, and arrived at ' the Forks ' on July 5. In Montreal he had formed the opinion that Lord Selkirk was a domineering autocrat. Now, however, he concluded after inquiry that Selkirk was neither irrational nor self-seeking, and advised that the accusations against him should not be brought into the courts. At the same time he bound Selkirk under bail of £10,000 to appear in Canada for trial. When Coltman returned to Lower Canada in the autumn of 1817, Sherbrooke was able to write the Colonial Office that ' a degree of tranquility ' had been restored to the Indian Territories.

While in the west Lord Selkirk had gained the respect of the Indians, and in token of their admiration they gave him the unusual name of the ' Silver Chief.' Selkirk was anxious to extinguish the ancient title which the Indians had to the lands of Assiniboia, in order to prevent future disputes. To effect this he brought together at Fort

Douglas a body of chiefs who represented the Cree and Saulteaux nations. The Indian chiefs made eloquent speeches. They said that they were willing to surrender their claim to a strip on either side of the Red River up-stream from its mouth as far as the Red Lake river (now Grand Forks, North Dakota), and on either side of the Assiniboine as far as its junction with the Muskrat. Selkirk's desire was to obtain as much on each bank of these streams for the length agreed upon as could be seen under a horse's belly towards the horizon, or approximately two miles, and the Indians agreed. At three places— at Fort Douglas, Fort Daer, and the confluence of the Red and Red Lake rivers— Selkirk wished to secure about six miles on each side of the Red River, and to this the chiefs agreed. In the end, on July 18, 1817, Selkirk concluded a treaty, after distributing presents. It was the first treaty made by a subject of Great Britain with the tribes of Rupert's Land. In signing it the several chiefs drew odd pictures of animals on a rough map of the territory in question. These animals were their respective totems and were placed opposite the regions over which they claimed authority. It was stipulated that one hundred pounds of good tobacco should be given annually to each nation.

Having finished his work, Lord Selkirk bade the colony adieu and journeyed southward. He made his way through the unorganized territories which had belonged to the United States since the Louisiana Purchase of 1803, and at length reached the town of St Louis on the Mississippi. Thence he proceeded to the New England States, and by way of Albany reached the province of Upper Canada. Here he found that the agents of the North-West Company had been busy with plans to attack him in the courts. There were four charges against him, and he was ordered to appear at Sandwich, a judicial centre on the Detroit. The accusations related to his procedure at Fort William. Selkirk travelled to Sandwich. One of the charges was quickly dismissed. The other three were held over, pending the arrival of witnesses, and he was released on bail to the amount of £350.

In May 1818 Colin Robertson and several others were charged at Montreal with the wilful destruction of Fort Gibraltar, but the jury would not convict the accused upon the evidence presented. In September, at the judicial sessions at Sandwich, Lord Selkirk was again faced with charges. A legal celebrity of the day, Chief Justice Dummer Powell, presided. The grand jury complained that John Beverley Robinson, the attorney-general of the province, was interfering with their deliberations, and they refused to make a presentment. Chief Justice Powell waited two days for their answer, and as it was not forthcoming he adjourned the case. The actions were afterwards taken to York and were tried there. For some reason the leaders of the political faction known in the annals of Upper Canada as the Family Compact were not friendly to Lord Selkirk ; the Rev. John Strachan, the father-confessor of this group of politicians, was an open opponent. As a result of the trials Selkirk was mulcted in damages to the extent of £2000.

The courts of Lower Canada alone were empowered to deal with offences in the Indian Territories. The governor-general of Canada could, however, transfer the trial of such cases to Upper Canada, if he saw fit. This had been done in the case of the charges against Selkirk, and Sir John Sherbrooke, after consulting with the home authorities, decided to refer Selkirk's charges against the Nor'westers, in connection with the events of 1815 and 1816 on the Red River, to the court of the King's Bench at its autumn sitting in York. Beginning in October 1818, there were successive trials of persons accused by Lord Selkirk of various crimes. The cases were heard by Chief Justice Powell, assisted by Judges Boulton and Campbell. The evidence in regard to the massacre at Seven Oaks was full of interest. A passage from the speech of one of the counsel for the defence shows the ideas then current in Canada as to the value of the prairie country. Sherwood, one of the counsel, emphatically declared that Robert Semple was not a governor; he was an emperor. ' Yes, gentlemen,' reiterated Sherwood, his voice rising, ' I repeat, an emperor—a bashaw in that land of milk and honey, where nothing, not even a blade of corn, will ripen.' The result of the trials was disheartening to Selkirk. Of the various prisoners who were accused not one was found guilty.

Lord Selkirk did not attend the trials of the Nor'westers at York, and seems to have returned to Britain with his wife and children before the end of the year 1818. He was ill and in a most melancholy state of mind.

Unquestionably, he had not secured a full measure of justice in the courts of Canada. A man strong in health might have borne his misfortunes more lightly. As it was, Selkirk let his wrongs prey upon his spirit. On March 19, 1819, he addressed a letter to Lord Liverpool, asking that the Privy Council should intervene in order to correct the erroneous findings of the Canadian courts. Sir James Montgomery, Selkirk's brother-in-law, moved in the House of Commons, on June 24, that all official correspondence touching Selkirk's affairs should be produced. The result was the publication of a large blue-book. An effort was made to induce Sir Walter Scott to use his literary talents on his friend's behalf. But at the time Scott was prostrate with illness and unable to help the friend of his youth.

Meanwhile, Lord Selkirk's attachment for his colony on the Red River had not undergone any change. One of the last acts of his life was to seek settlers in Switzerland, and a considerable number of Swiss families were persuaded to migrate to Assiniboia. But the heads of these families were not fitted for pioneer life on the prairie. For the most part they were poor musicians, pastry-cooks, clockmakers, and the like, who knew nothing of husbandry. Their chief contribution to the colony was a number of buxom, red-cheeked daughters, whose arrival in 1821 created a joyful commotion among the military bachelors at the settlement. The fair newcomers were quickly wooed and won by the men who had served in Napoleon's wars, and numerous marriages followed.

Selkirk's continued ill-health caused him to seek the temperate climate of the south of France, and there he died on April 8, 1820, at Pau, in the foothills of the Pyrenees. His body was taken to Orthez, a small town some twenty-five miles away, and buried there in the Protestant cemetery. The length of two countries separates Lord Selkirk's place of burial from his place of birth. He has a monument in Scotland and a monument in France, but his most enduring monument is the great Canadian West of which he was the true founder. His only son, Dunbar James Douglas, inherited the title, and when he died in 1885 the line of Selkirk became extinct. Long before this the Selkirk family had broken the tie with the Canadian West. In 1836 their rights in the country of Assiniboia, in so far as it lay in British territory, were purchased by the Hudson's Bay Company for the sum of £84,000.

The character of the fifth Earl of Selkirk has been alike lauded and vilified. Shortly after his death the *Gentleman's Magazine* commended his benefactions to the poor and his kindness as a landlord. ' To the counsels of an enlightened philosophy and an immovable firmness of purpose,' declared the writer, ' he added the most complete habits of business and a perfect knowledge of affairs.' Sir Walter Scott wrote of Selkirk with abundant fervour. ' I never knew in my life,' said the Wizard of the North, ' a man of a more generous and disinterested disposition, or one whose talents and perseverance were better qualified to bring great and national schemes to conclusion.' History has proved that Lord Selkirk was a man of dreams; it is false to say, however, that his were fruitless visions. Time has fully justified his colonizing activity in relation to settlement on the Red River. He was firmly convinced of what few in his day believed—that the soil of the prairie was fruitful and would give bread to the sower. His worst fault was his partisanship. In his eyes the Hudson's Bay Company was endowed with all the virtues ; and he never properly analysed the motives or recognized the achievements of its great rival. Had he but ordered his representatives in Assiniboia to meet the Nor'westers half-way, distress and hardship might have been lessened, and violence might very probably have been entirely avoided.

The presence of Lord Selkirk on the Red River had led to renewed energy on the part of the colonists. They began to till the land, and in 1818 the grain and vegetable crops promised an abundant yield. In July, however, when the time of harvest was approaching, the settlers experienced a calamity that brought poverty for the present and despair for the future. The sky was suddenly darkened by a great cloud of locusts, which had come from their breeding-places in the far south-west. During a single night, 'crops, gardens, and every green herb in the settlement had perished, with the exception of a few ears of barley gleaned in the women's aprons.' In the following year the plague reappeared ; the insects came again, covering the ground so thickly that they 'might be shovelled with a spade.' The stock of seed-grain was now almost exhausted, and the colonists resolved to send an expedition to the Mississippi for a fresh supply. Two hundred and fifty bushels of grain were secured at Lord Selkirk's expense, and brought back on flat-boats to the colony. Never since that time has there been a serious lack of seed on the Red River.

The year 1821 brings us to a milestone in the history of the Canadian West, and at this point our story terminates. After Lord Selkirk's death the two great fur-trading companies realized the folly of continuing their disastrous rivalry, and made prepara-tions to bury their differences. Neither com-pany had been making satisfactory profits. In Great Britain especially, where only the echoes of the struggle had been heard, was there an increasing desire that the two com-panies should unite. One of the foremost partners of the North-West Company was Edward Ellice, a native of Aberdeenshire, and member of the House of Commons for Coventry. Ellice championed the party among the Nor'westers who were in favour of union, and the two M'Gillivrays, Simon and William, earnestly seconded his efforts. Terms acceptable to both companies were at length agreed upon. On March 26, 1821, a formal document, called a ' deed-poll,' outlining the basis of union, was signed by the two parties

in London. In 1822 Edward Ellice intro-
duced a bill in parliament making the union of
the companies legal. The name of the North-
West Company was dropped; the new cor-
poration was to be known as the Hudson's
Bay Company. Thus passed away for ever
the singular partnership of the North-West
Company which had made Montreal a market
for furs and had built up Fort William in
the depths of the forest. No longer did two
rival trading-posts stand by lake or stream.
No longer did two rival camp-fires light up
blazed tree-trunk or grass-strewn prairie by
the long and sinuous trail. From Labrador
to Vancouver, and from the Arctic to the
southern confines of the Canadian West and
farther, the British flag, with H. B. C. on its
folds, was to wave over every trading-post.
Midway between the Atlantic and the Pacific
a little hamlet was to struggle into life, to
struggle feebly for many years—a mere
adjunct of a fur-trading post; but at length
it was to come into its own, and Winnipeg,
the proudest city of the plains, was in time to
rear its palaces on the spot where for long
years the Red River Colony battled for existence against human enemies and the obstacles
of nature.

BIBLIOGRAPHICAL NOTE

PRIMARY SOURCES

THE Selkirk Papers in the Dominion Archives consist of seventy-nine portfolios containing transcripts of correspondence, legal evidence, and other proceedings relating to the Earl of Selkirk's colonizing enterprises.

Lord Selkirk's principal works are: *Observations on the Present State of the Highlands in Scotland* (published in 1805 and describing the journey to Prince Edward Island, etc., in 1803) ; *On the Necessity of a more Efficient System of National Defence* (1808) ; *A Sketch of the British Fur Trade in North America* (1816).

The Letter Book of Miles Macdonell—July 27, 1811, to February 25, 1812 (Dominion Archives Report, 1886)—contains ten letters addressed by Macdonell to Selkirk from Yarmouth, Stornoway, York Factory, and Nelson Encampment; besides others to various individuals.

In consequence of the disasters which befell the Red River Colony in 1815 and 1816, there appeared in Great Britain *A Statement respecting the Earl of Selkirk's Settlement upon the Red River in North America, etc.* (republished by John Murray,

London, 1817). In answer to this the North-West Company put forth *A Narrative of Occurrences in the Indian Countries, etc.* (1817), to which were appended twenty-nine documents to substantiate claims made. These works, although written in a partisan spirit, contain information which cannot be had from any other source.

The following are also useful: John M'Leod's Diary, 1815; Letter of Cuthbert Grant to J. D. Cameron, March 13, 1816; North-West Company's Account Book for Fort Gibraltar, 1815; Governor Macdonell's Proclamation, January 1814; Charter of the Hudson's Bay Company; Colonel W. B. Coltman's Report, 1817; A. Amos, *Report of the Trials in the Courts of Canada relative to the Destruction of the Earl of Selkirk's Settlement on the Red River, with Observations* (1820); *Trials of the Earl of Selkirk against the North-West Company in 1818* (Montreal, 1819); Notices of the Claims of the Hudson's Bay Company, and the Conduct of its Adversaries (Montreal, 1817); Chief Justice Powell's Report *re* North-West Disputes (Dominion Archives Report, 1897); a pamphlet against Lord Selkirk by John Strachan, D.D. (1816), and the reply thereto by Archibald Macdonald (1816); the communications of 'Mercator' appearing in the Montreal *Herald* (1816); Bluebook on Red River Settlement (Imperial House of Commons, 1819); Original Letters regarding the Selkirk Settlement (Manitoba Historical and Scientific Society, 1889); Lord Selkirk's Treaty with the Western Indians (*vide* Appendix to *The Treaties of Canada* by Alexander Morris, 1880).

SECONDARY MATERIAL

Since the present story closes with 1821, it is necessary to classify as secondary material a work that is to be regarded as a primary source on the later history of the colony—*The Red River Settlement* (1856) by Alexander Ross. Ross was a pioneer emigrant to the colony of Astoria on the Pacific Coast. In 1817 he entered the service of the North-West Company; after the union of the fur companies in 1821 he remained in the employ of the Hudson's Bay Company. In 1825 he went as a settler to the Red River Colony, where he soon became an influential officer. His narrative is vigorous in style as well as fair-minded in its criticisms, and is an indispensable authority on the beginnings of Manitoba.

The most prolific writer upon the career of Lord Selkirk and the history of the Red River Colony is Professor George Bryce, of Winnipeg, who has been a resident at 'the Forks' of the Red and Assiniboine rivers since 1871. He has thus been in a position to gather and preserve the traditions handed down by redskin, trapper, and colonist. Consult his *Romantic Settlement of Lord Selkirk's Colonists* (1909); also *Manitoba: Infancy, Progress and Present Condition* (1872); *The Remarkable History of the Hudson's Bay Company* (1900); *Mackenzie, Selkirk and Simpson* (1906).

An account of Lord Selkirk will be found in Kingsford, *History of Canada*, vol. ix. The reader should also consult, in *Canada and its Provinces* (vol. xix), the excellent monograph by Professor Chester Martin. This is the most recent and probably the most thoroughly grounded study of the Red River Colony. The same work contains a good account of the Selkirk Settlement in Prince Edward Island (vol. xiii, p. 354) by Dr Andrew Macphail. The Baldoon Settlement is treated of by Dr George W. Mitchell in the *Proceedings of the Ontario Historical Society* for 1913. See also the monograph, 'Pioneer Settlements' [of Upper Canada], by A. C. Casselman in *Canada and its Provinces*, vol. xvii.

INDEX

147

Printed by T. and A. Constable, Printers to His Majesty at the Edinburgh University Press

Breinigsville, PA USA
04 April 2011
259106BV00004B/6/P